KENTACHI

MONICA CIABATTINI

Kentachi was originally published in Italy by Zen Comics

Monica Ciabattini
Story, Pencils, Inks and Colour

Gianluca Testaverde
Publisher

Andrea Pinto
Editor In Chief

Maria Lidia Linari
English Translation

FOR MARKOSIA ENTERPRISES LTD

HARRY MARKOS
PUBLISHER + MANAGING PARTNER

GM JORDAN
SPECIAL PROJECTS CO-ORDINATOR

ANDY BRIGGS
CREATIVE CONSULTANT

IAN SHARMAN
EDITOR IN CHIEF

www.markosia.com

 Published by Markosia Enterprises, PO BOX 3477, Barnet, Hertfordshire, EN5 9HN. FIRST PRINTING, February 2024. Harry Markos, Director.

ISBN 978-1-916968-26-4

www.markosia.com

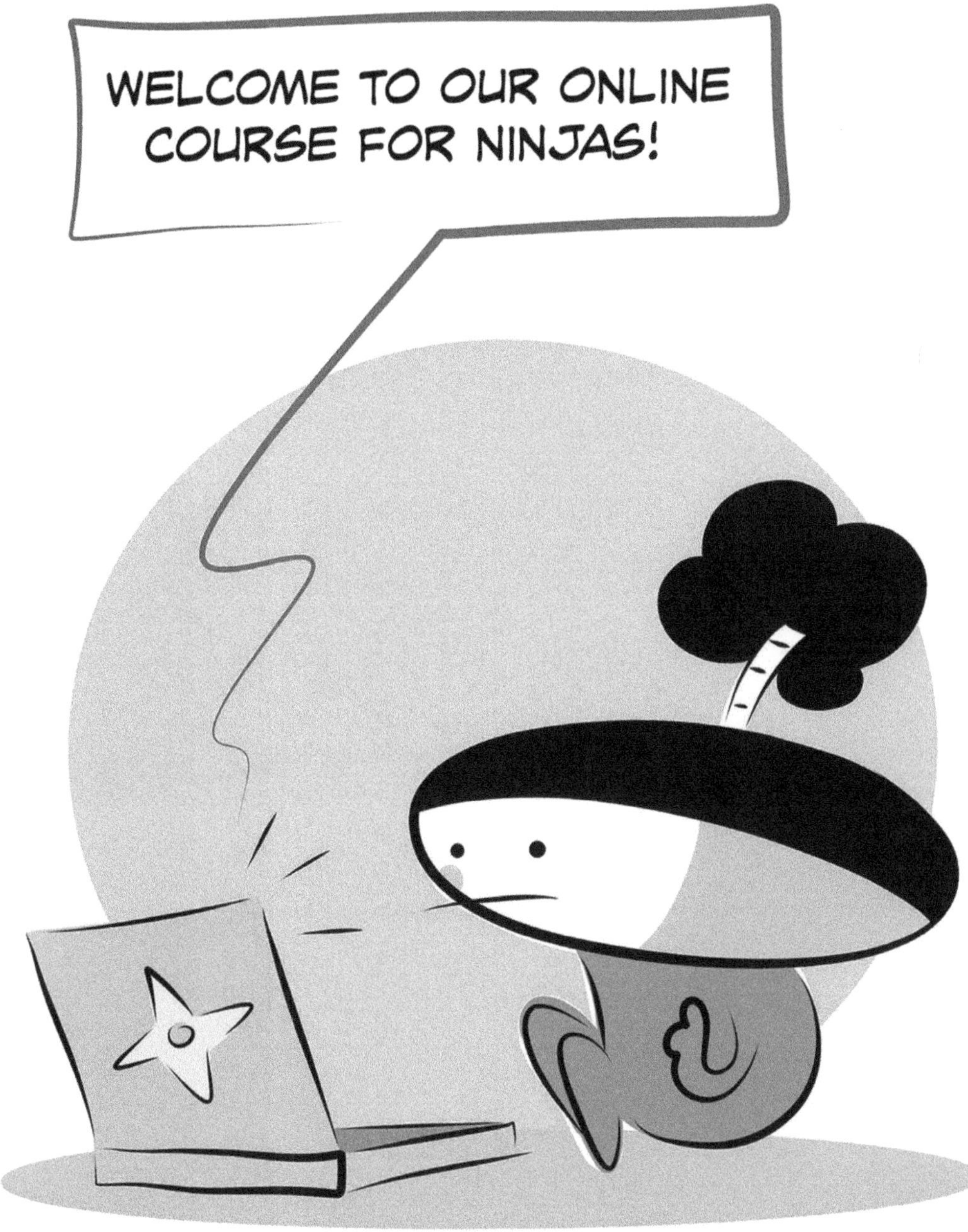
WELCOME TO OUR ONLINE COURSE FOR NINJAS!

THE BRIEF STORY OF KENTACHI

IT WAS A DAY LIKE ANY OTHER WHEN LITTLE KENTACHI WAS ABANDONED BY MISTAKE BY HIS PARENTS, WHO LEFT TO BUY A JAR OF SARDINIAN CHILI!

MASTER PAKURO SARUTORY WAS ON HIS WAY TO PICK APPLES TO MAKE A SMOOTHIE...

AND THAT'S WHEN HE SUDDENTLY SAW A BASKET WITH A BABY INSIDE!

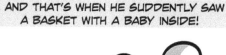

HE DECIDED TO TAKE CARE OF HIM, WISHING TO MAKE A GREAT NINJA OUT OF HIM!

CAN I EAT HIM?

NO!

END

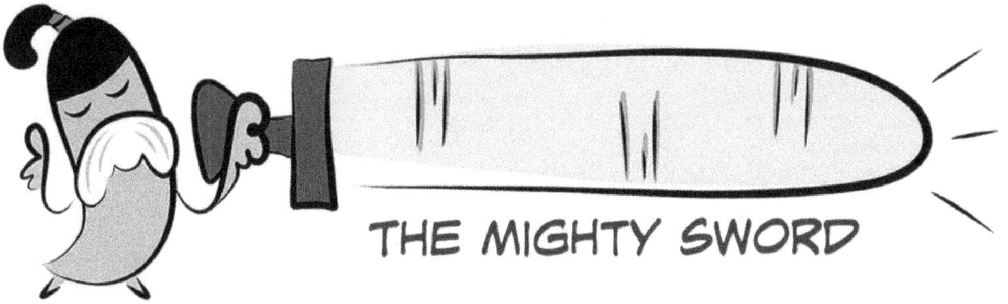

THE MIGHTY SWORD

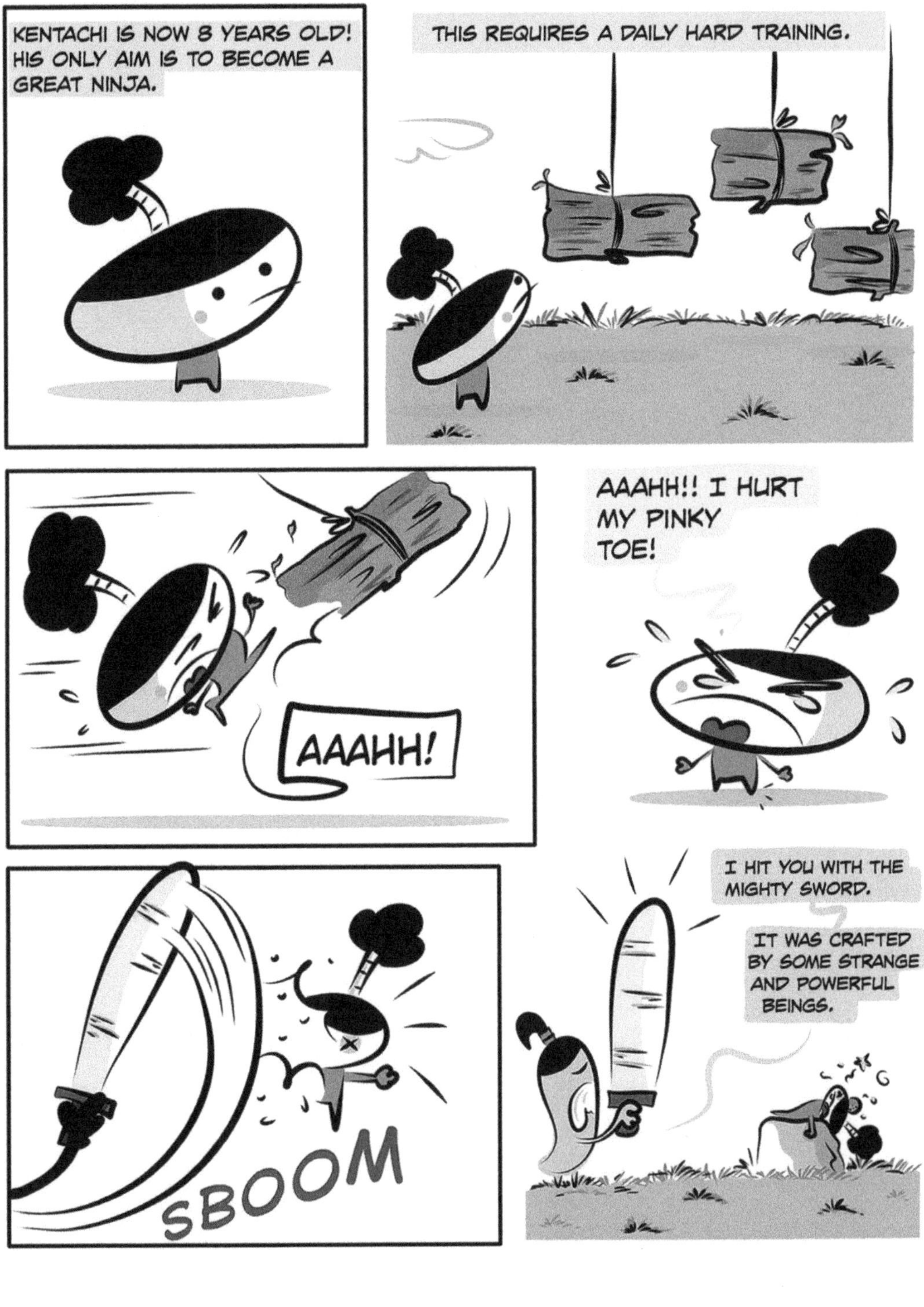
KENTACHI IS NOW 8 YEARS OLD! HIS ONLY AIM IS TO BECOME A GREAT NINJA.
THIS REQUIRES A DAILY HARD TRAINING.
AAAHH!
AAAHH!! I HURT MY PINKY TOE!
SBOOM
I HIT YOU WITH THE MIGHTY SWORD.
IT WAS CRAFTED BY SOME STRANGE AND POWERFUL BEINGS.

AN ANCIENT TO-
WER KEPT THE
SECRET OF THIS
SWORD FOR
CENTURIES.

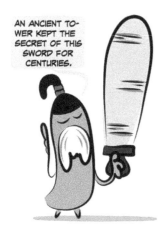

IN FRONT OF THAT TO-
WER, THERE WAS A
SNAKE ON WATCH.

BUT THESE WEIRD CREA-
TURES WHO CAME FROM
PLANET PLUF-PLOF MA-
NAGED TO STEAL IT AND
TO BOOST ITS POWER.

GIVE US THAT SWORD,
IF YOU DON'T WANT
TO LOSE YOUR FA-
MILY!

THAT'S FINE, YOU
CAN TAKE IT

THE SNAKE REMEMBERED
TOO LATE THAT HE HAD
NO FAMILY.

SIGH!

AND THAT'S
WHEN I ARRIVED!

THESE CREATURES LO-
VED CANDIES...

I GAVE THEM SO MANY
THAT THEY HAD TO LOOK
FOR A DENTIST TO CURE
THEIR TOOTHACHE. AND THEN
I TOOK THE SWORD!

YOU ARE TOO COOL,
MASTER.

CAN I WIELD IT
TOO ONE
DAY?

NO!

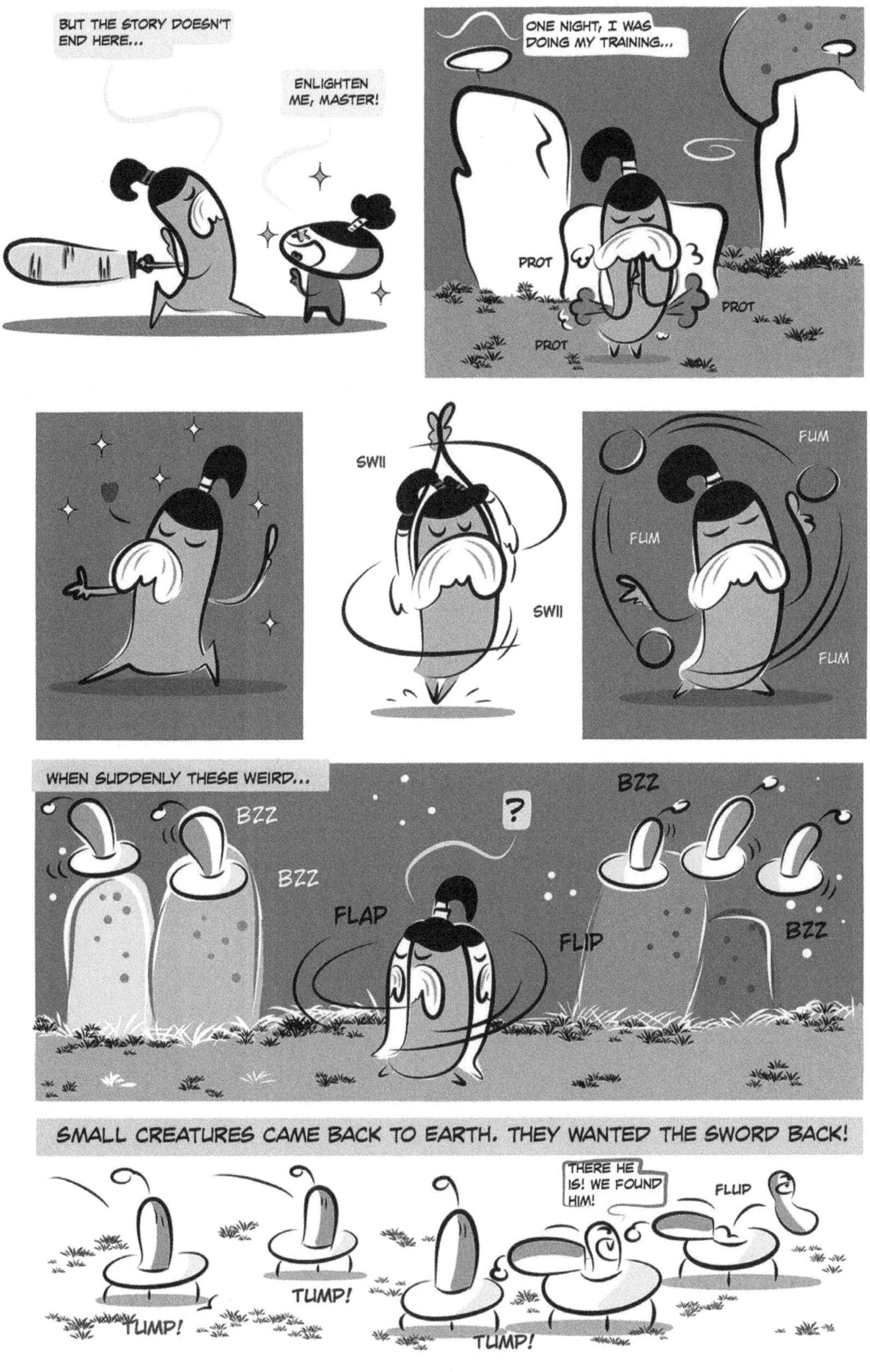
BUT THE STORY DOESN'T END HERE...
ENLIGHTEN ME, MASTER!
ONE NIGHT, I WAS DOING MY TRAINING...
PROT
PROT
PROT
SWII
SWII
FUM
FUM
FUM
WHEN SUDDENLY THESE WEIRD...
BZZ
BZZ
?
BZZ
FLAP
FLIP
BZZ
SMALL CREATURES CAME BACK TO EARTH. THEY WANTED THE SWORD BACK!
THERE HE IS! WE FOUND HIM!
FLUP
TUMP!
TUMP!
TUMP!

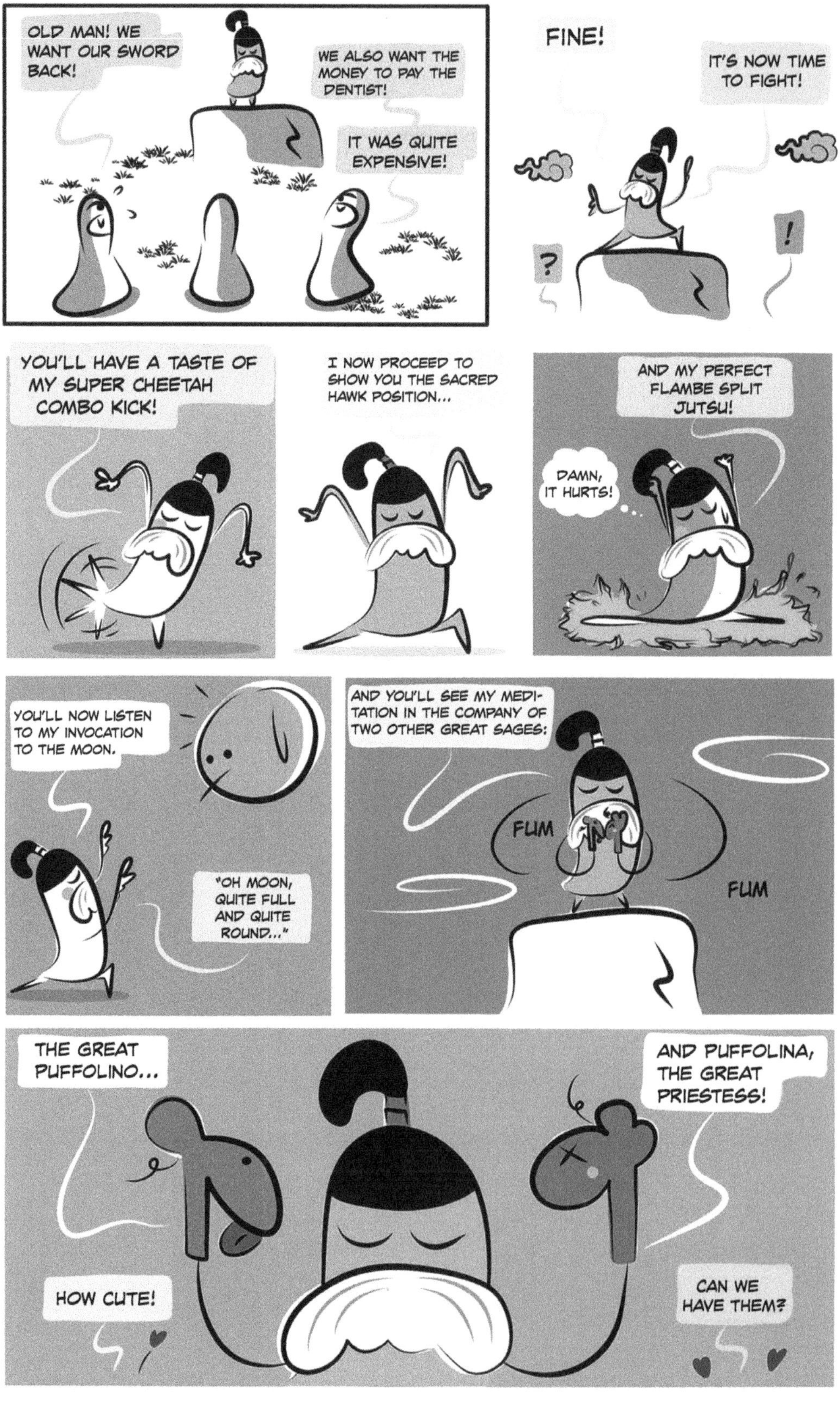
OLD MAN! WE WANT OUR SWORD BACK!
WE ALSO WANT THE MONEY TO PAY THE DENTIST!
IT WAS QUITE EXPENSIVE!
FINE!
IT'S NOW TIME TO FIGHT!
?
!
YOU'LL HAVE A TASTE OF MY SUPER CHEETAH COMBO KICK!
I NOW PROCEED TO SHOW YOU THE SACRED HAWK POSITION...
AND MY PERFECT FLAMBE SPLIT JUTSU!
DAMN, IT HURTS!
YOU'LL NOW LISTEN TO MY INVOCATION TO THE MOON.
"OH MOON, QUITE FULL AND QUITE ROUND..."
AND YOU'LL SEE MY MEDITATION IN THE COMPANY OF TWO OTHER GREAT SAGES:
FUM
FUM
THE GREAT PUFFOLINO...
AND PUFFOLINA, THE GREAT PRIESTESS!
HOW CUTE!
CAN WE HAVE THEM?

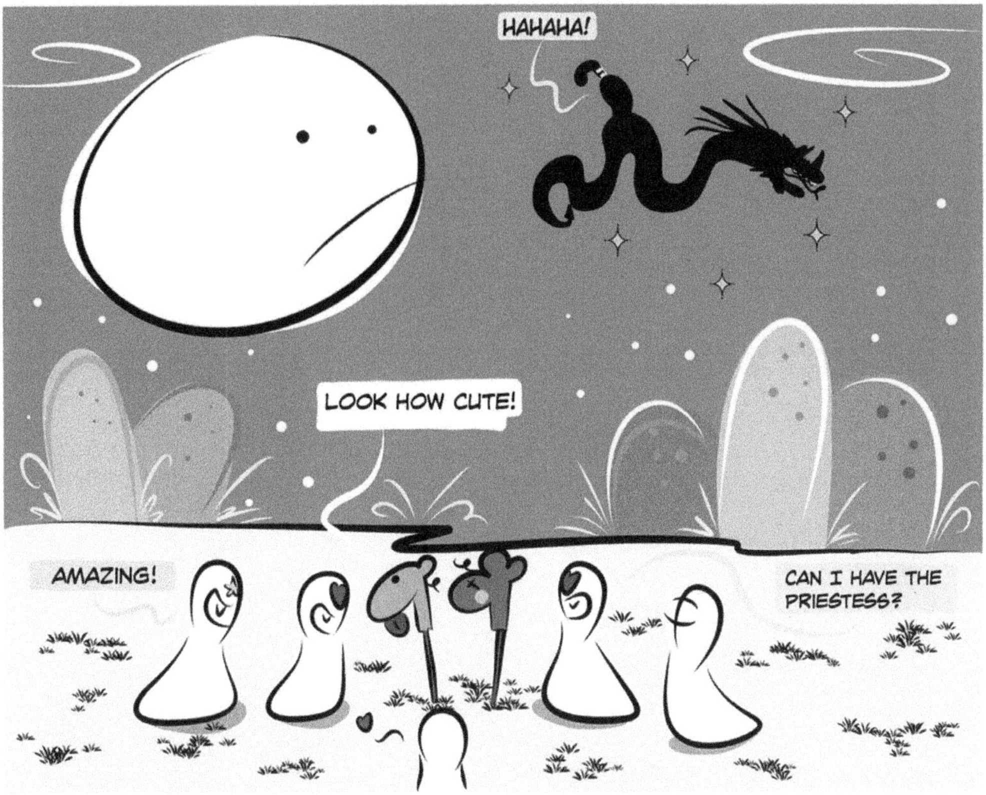
HAHAHA!
LOOK HOW CUTE!
AMAZING!
CAN I HAVE THE PRIESTESS?

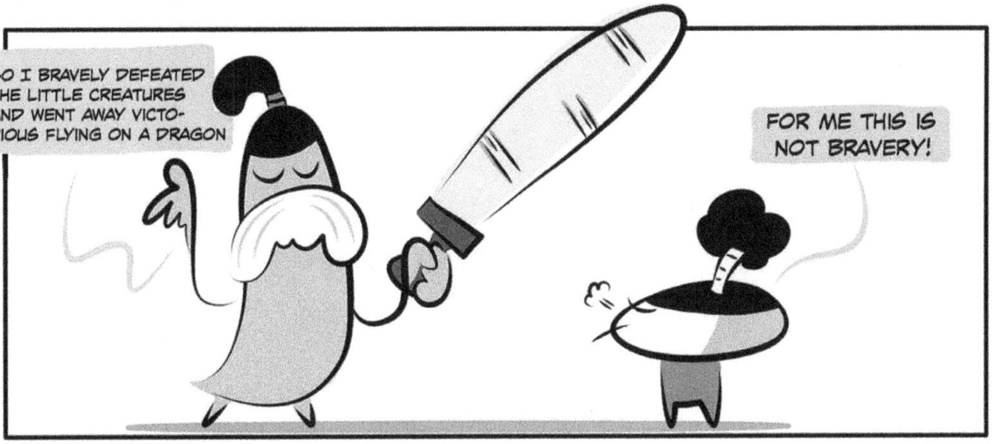
SO I BRAVELY DEFEATED THE LITTLE CREATURES AND WENT AWAY VICTORIOUS FLYING ON A DRAGON
FOR ME THIS IS NOT BRAVERY!

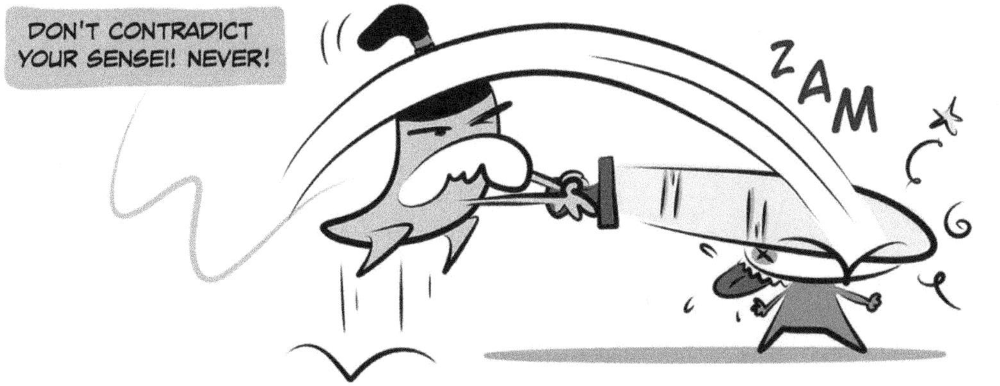
DON'T CONTRADICT YOUR SENSEI! NEVER!
ZAM

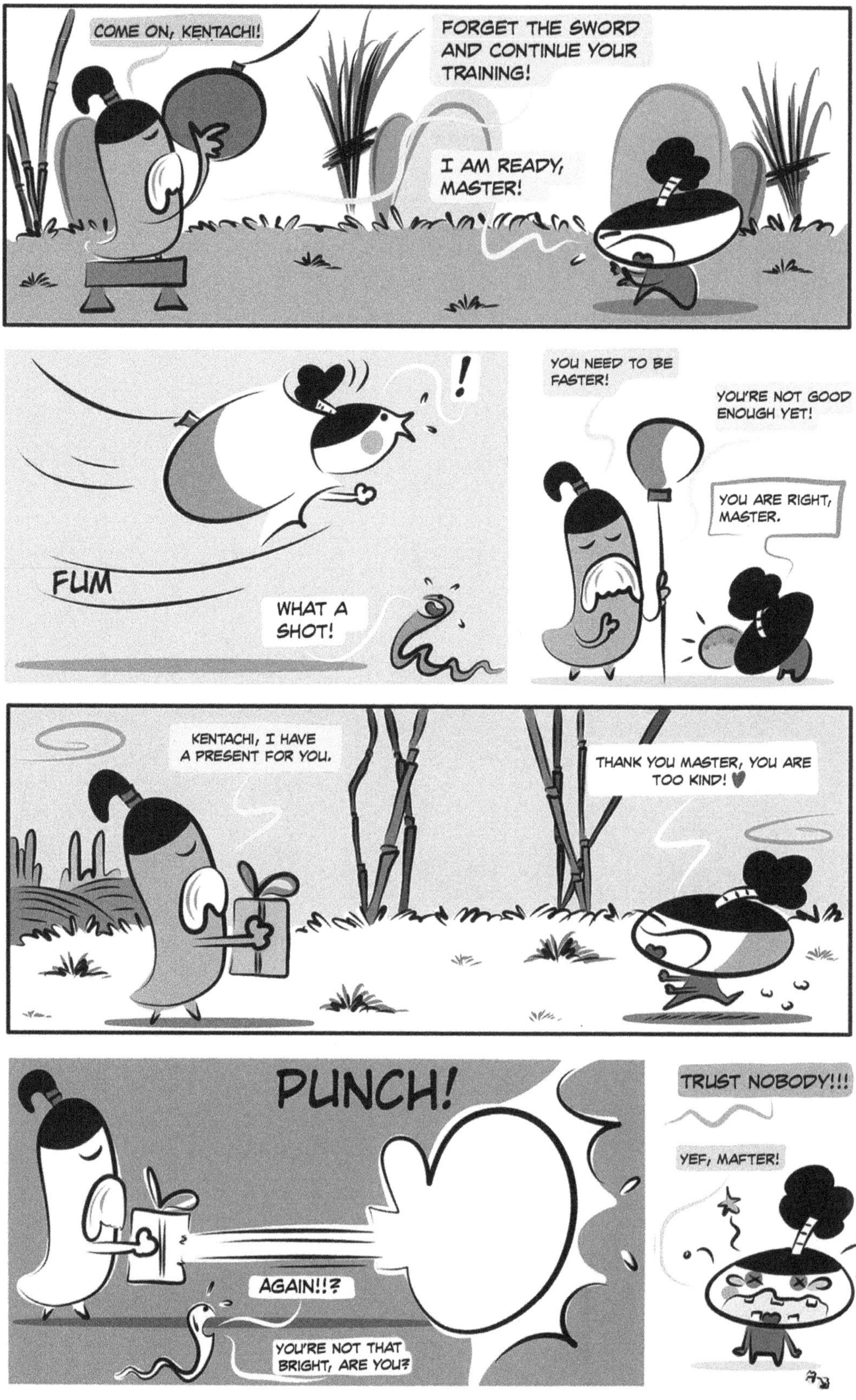
COME ON, KENTACHI!
FORGET THE SWORD AND CONTINUE YOUR TRAINING!
I AM READY, MASTER!
FUM
WHAT A SHOT!
YOU NEED TO BE FASTER!
YOU'RE NOT GOOD ENOUGH YET!
YOU ARE RIGHT, MASTER.
KENTACHI, I HAVE A PRESENT FOR YOU.
THANK YOU MASTER, YOU ARE TOO KIND!
PUNCH!
AGAIN!!?
YOU'RE NOT THAT BRIGHT, ARE YOU?
TRUST NOBODY!!!
YEF, MAFTER!

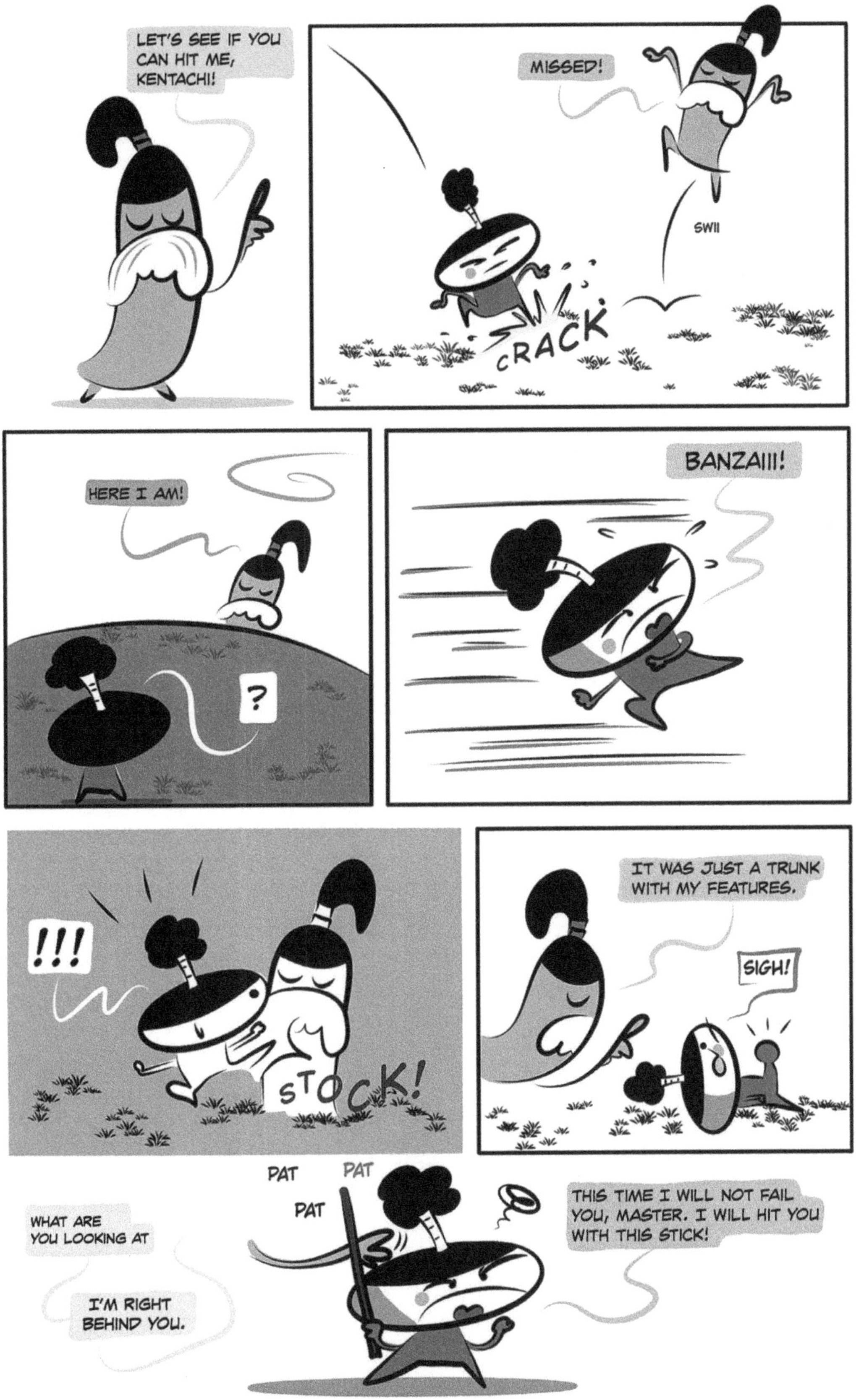
LET'S SEE IF YOU CAN HIT ME, KENTACHI!
MISSED!
SWII
CRACK
HERE I AM!
?
BANZAIII!
!!!
STOCK!
IT WAS JUST A TRUNK WITH MY FEATURES.
SIGH!
WHAT ARE YOU LOOKING AT
I'M RIGHT BEHIND YOU.
PAT
PAT
PAT
THIS TIME I WILL NOT FAIL YOU, MASTER. I WILL HIT YOU WITH THIS STICK!

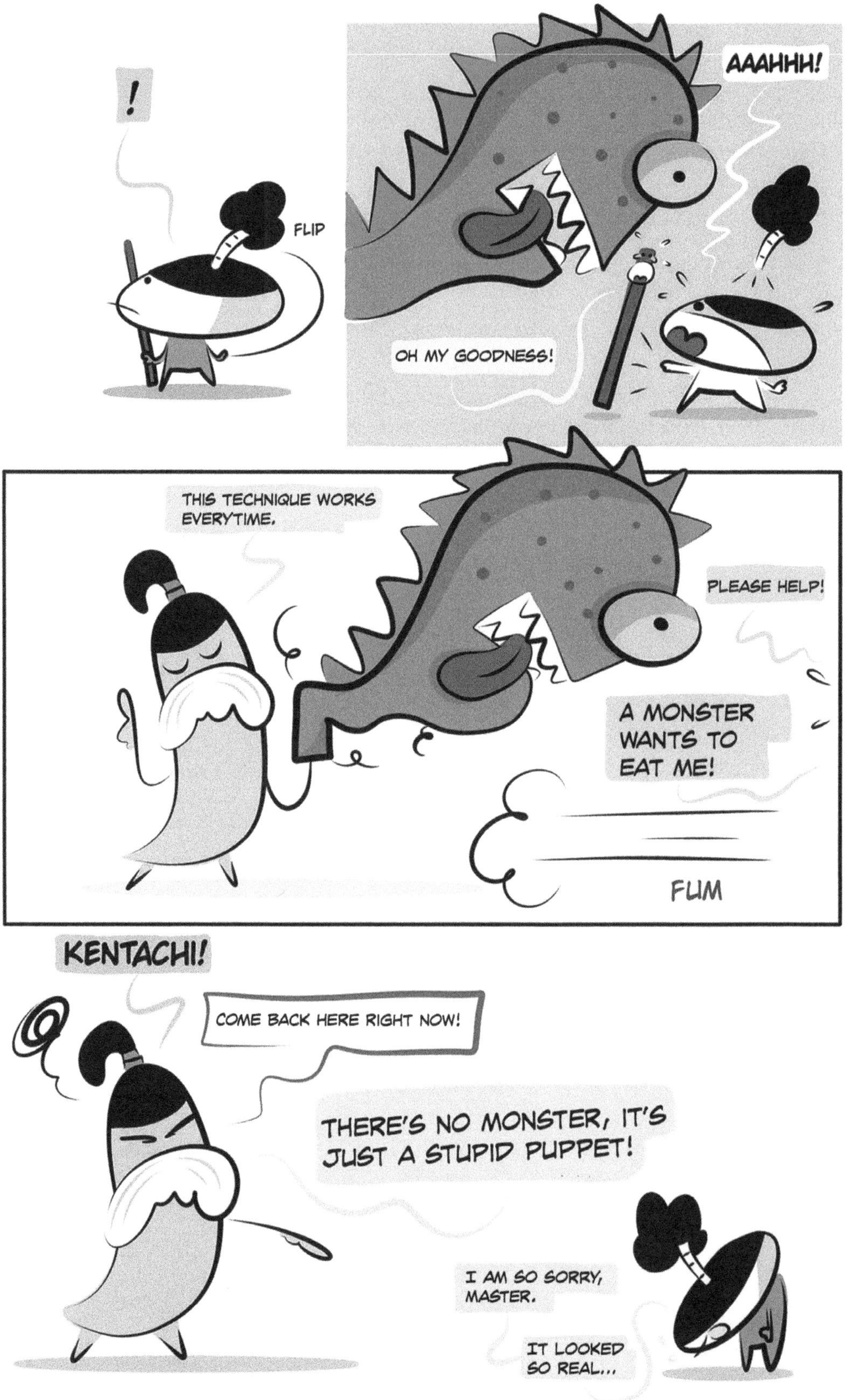
!
FLIP
AAAHHH!
OH MY GOODNESS!
THIS TECHNIQUE WORKS EVERYTIME.
PLEASE HELP!
A MONSTER WANTS TO EAT ME!
FUM
KENTACHI!
COME BACK HERE RIGHT NOW!
THERE'S NO MONSTER, IT'S JUST A STUPID PUPPET!
I AM SO SORRY, MASTER.
IT LOOKED SO REAL...

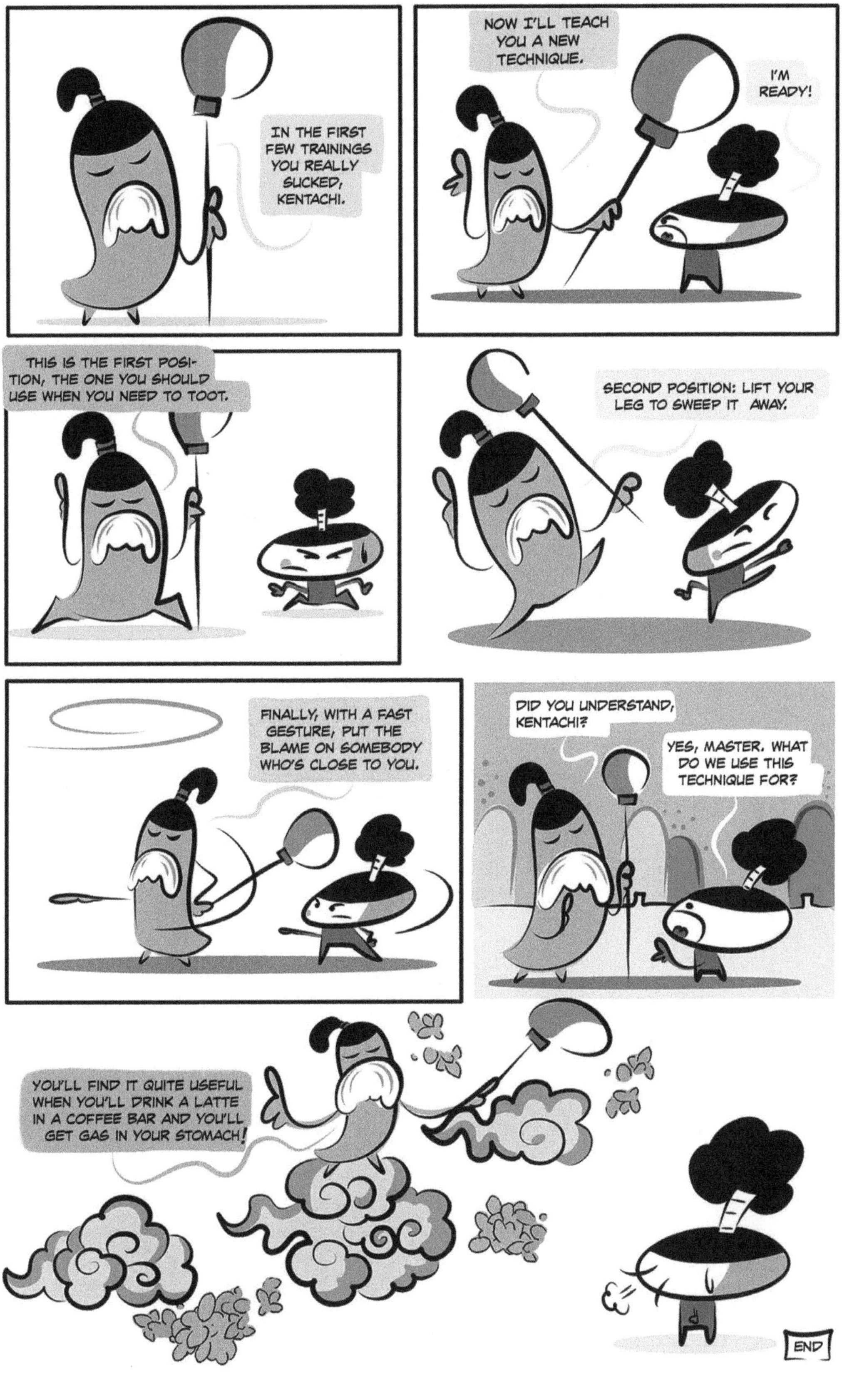
IN THE FIRST FEW TRAININGS YOU REALLY SUCKED, KENTACHI.
NOW I'LL TEACH YOU A NEW TECHNIQUE.
I'M READY!
THIS IS THE FIRST POSITION, THE ONE YOU SHOULD USE WHEN YOU NEED TO TOOT.
SECOND POSITION: LIFT YOUR LEG TO SWEEP IT AWAY.
FINALLY, WITH A FAST GESTURE, PUT THE BLAME ON SOMEBODY WHO'S CLOSE TO YOU.
DID YOU UNDERSTAND, KENTACHI?
YES, MASTER. WHAT DO WE USE THIS TECHNIQUE FOR?
YOU'LL FIND IT QUITE USEFUL WHEN YOU'LL DRINK A LATTE IN A COFFEE BAR AND YOU'LL GET GAS IN YOUR STOMACH!
END

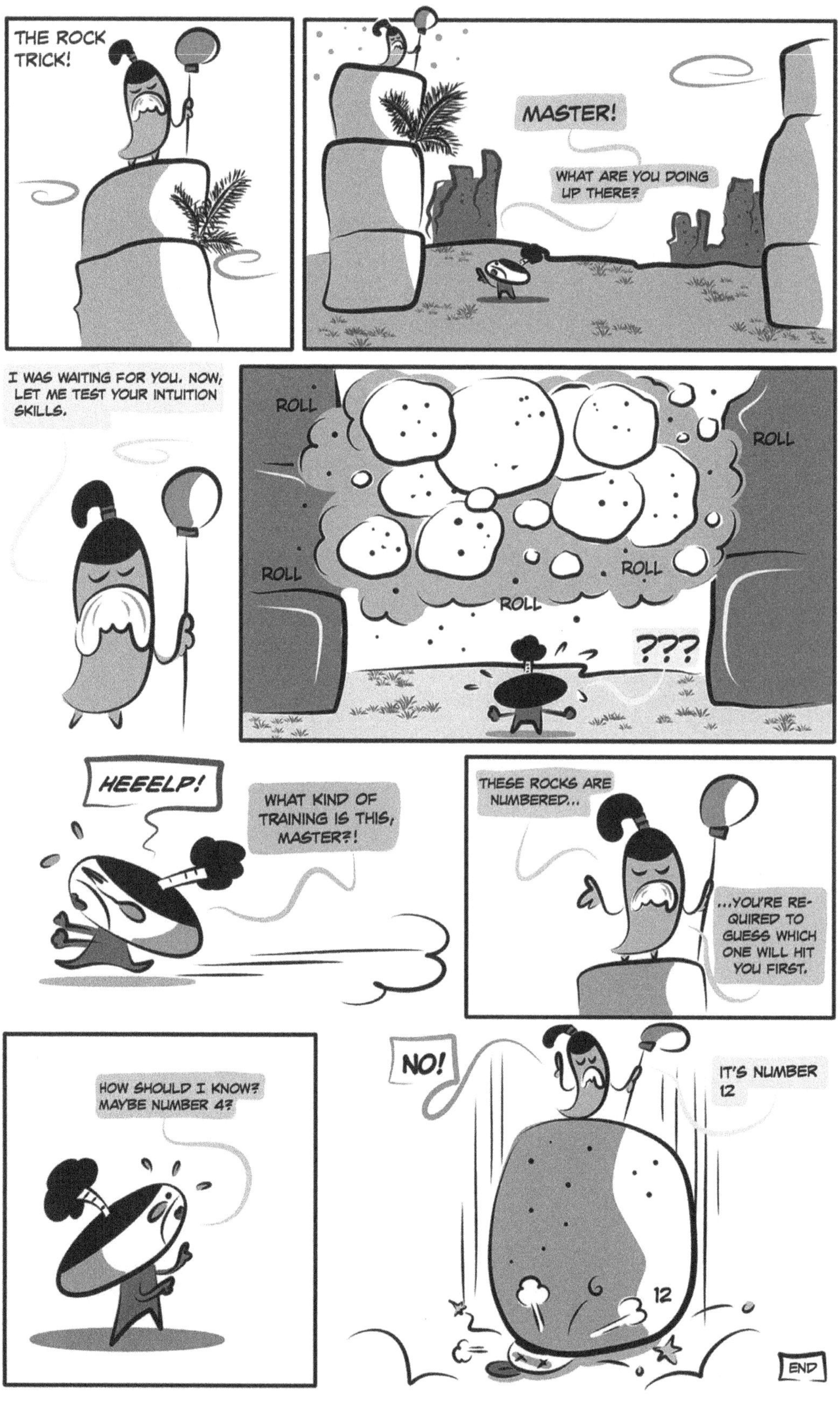
THE ROCK TRICK!
MASTER!
WHAT ARE YOU DOING UP THERE?
I WAS WAITING FOR YOU. NOW, LET ME TEST YOUR INTUITION SKILLS.
ROLL
ROLL
ROLL
ROLL
ROLL
???
HEEELP!
WHAT KIND OF TRAINING IS THIS, MASTER?!
THESE ROCKS ARE NUMBERED...
...YOU'RE RE-QUIRED TO GUESS WHICH ONE WILL HIT YOU FIRST.
HOW SHOULD I KNOW? MAYBE NUMBER 4?
NO!
IT'S NUMBER 12
12
END

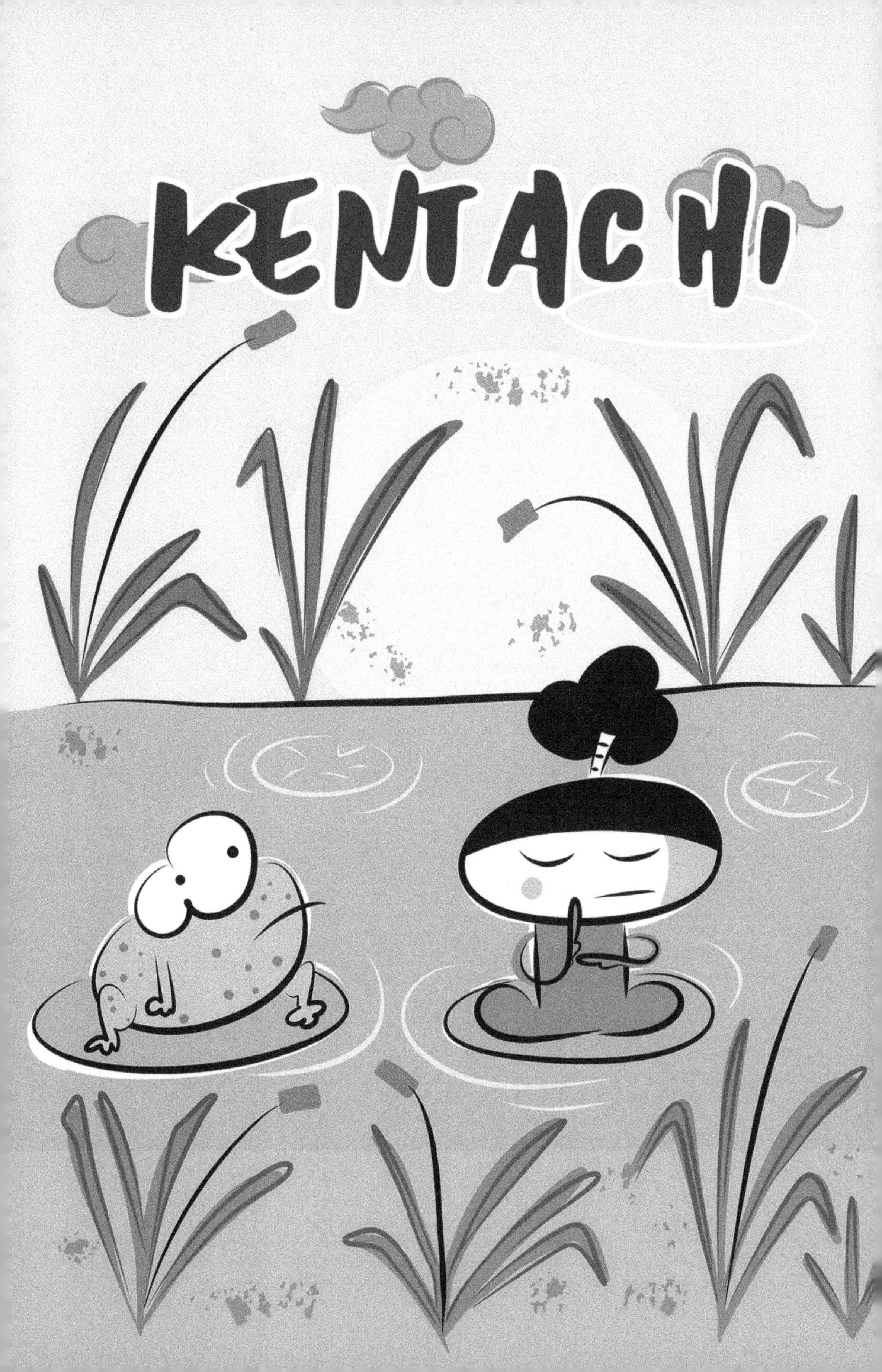
KENTACHI

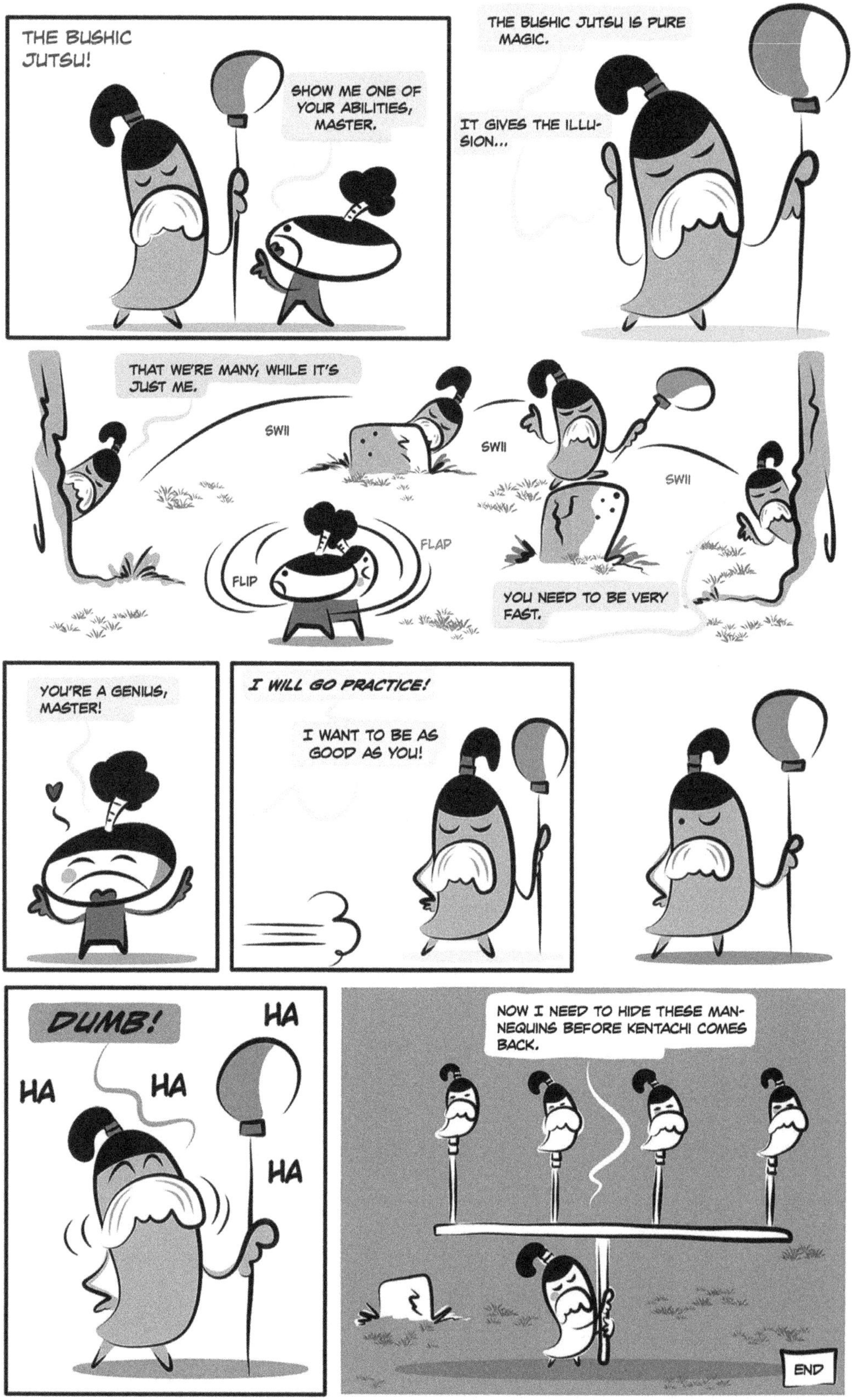
THE BUSHIC JUTSU!
SHOW ME ONE OF YOUR ABILITIES, MASTER.
THE BUSHIC JUTSU IS PURE MAGIC.
IT GIVES THE ILLU-SION...
THAT WE'RE MANY, WHILE IT'S JUST ME.
SWII
SWII
SWII
FLAP
FLIP
YOU NEED TO BE VERY FAST.
YOU'RE A GENIUS, MASTER!
I WILL GO PRACTICE!
I WANT TO BE AS GOOD AS YOU!
DUMB!
HA
HA
HA
HA
NOW I NEED TO HIDE THESE MAN-NEQUINS BEFORE KENTACHI COMES BACK.
END

THE RUN AWAY
JUTSU!

MASTER PAKURO AND KENTACHI ARE HAVING A WALK IN THE DESERT,
WHEN SUDDENLY...

ᵀUₘₚ!

MASTER PAKURO
SARUTORY, I WANT TO
FIGHT YOU!

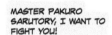

!

I SEE.

I'LL USE THIS KNIFE
CRAFTED BY MY
GRANDAD RIGHT BE-
FORE HE WENT
SHOPPING!

THIS FLOWER IS FOR YOU,
IT COMES FROM THE
MOUNTAIN OF GLORY.

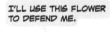

I'LL USE THIS FLOWER
TO DEFEND ME.

HOW DO YOU THINK
YOU CAN WIN WITH
A SIMPLE FLOWER?

HE'S
A GREAT MASTER,
BUT SOMETIMES
I JUST DON'T
GET IT.

HOW CAN YOU BE SO
STUPID?

WHY ARE WE RUNNING
AWAY? AND WHAT ARE
THESE WATERMELONS?

OH! THANK YOU, MASTER,
NOBODY EVER GAVE ME
SUCH A WONDERFUL FLOWER.

SHUT UP AND LISTEN
TO THE WATERMELONS'
ROLLING.

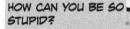

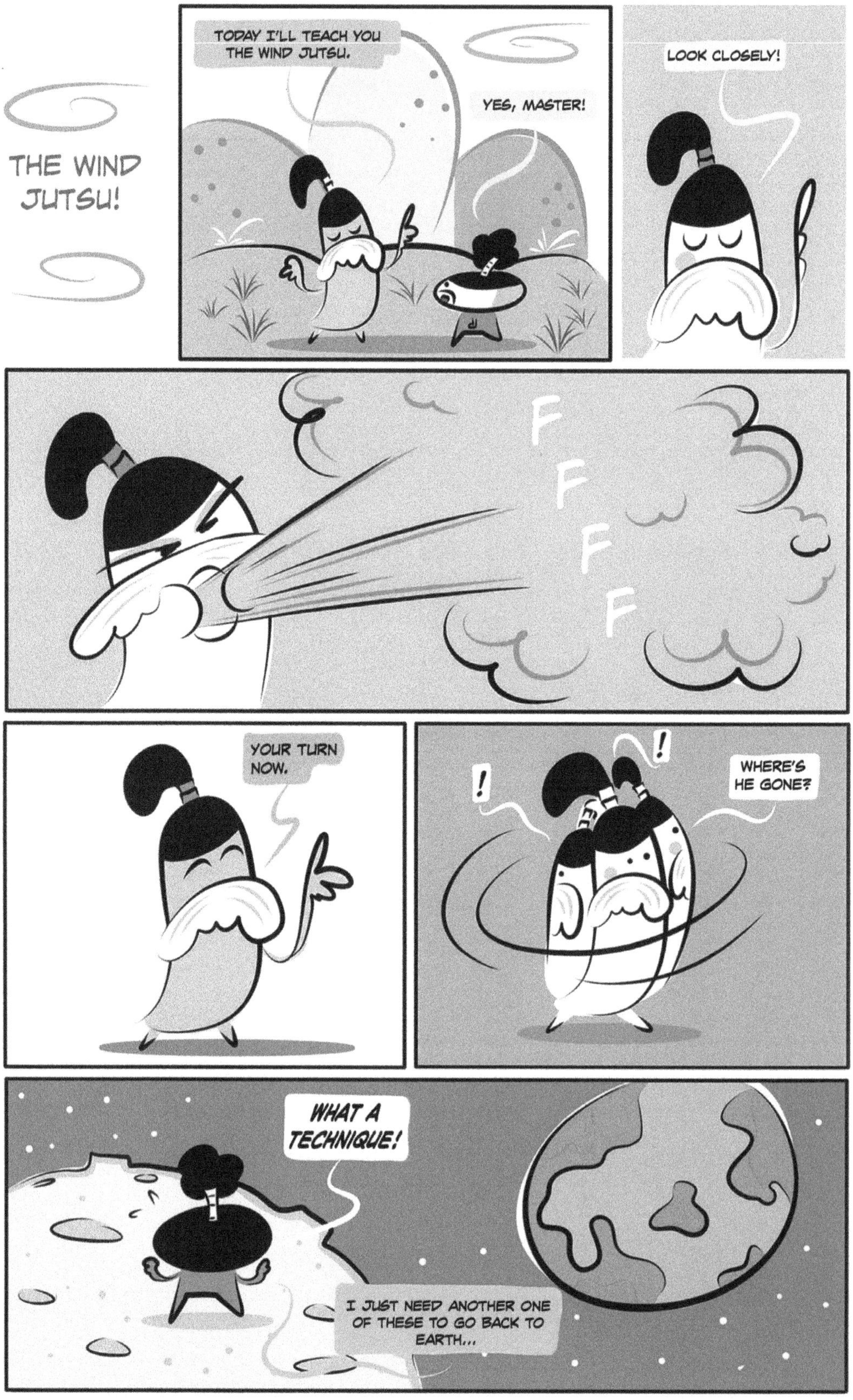
THE WIND JUTSU!
TODAY I'LL TEACH YOU THE WIND JUTSU.
YES, MASTER!
LOOK CLOSELY!
FFFF
YOUR TURN NOW.
!
!
WHERE'S HE GONE?
WHAT A TECHNIQUE!
I JUST NEED ANOTHER ONE OF THESE TO GO BACK TO EARTH...

THE EVIL PENGUIN

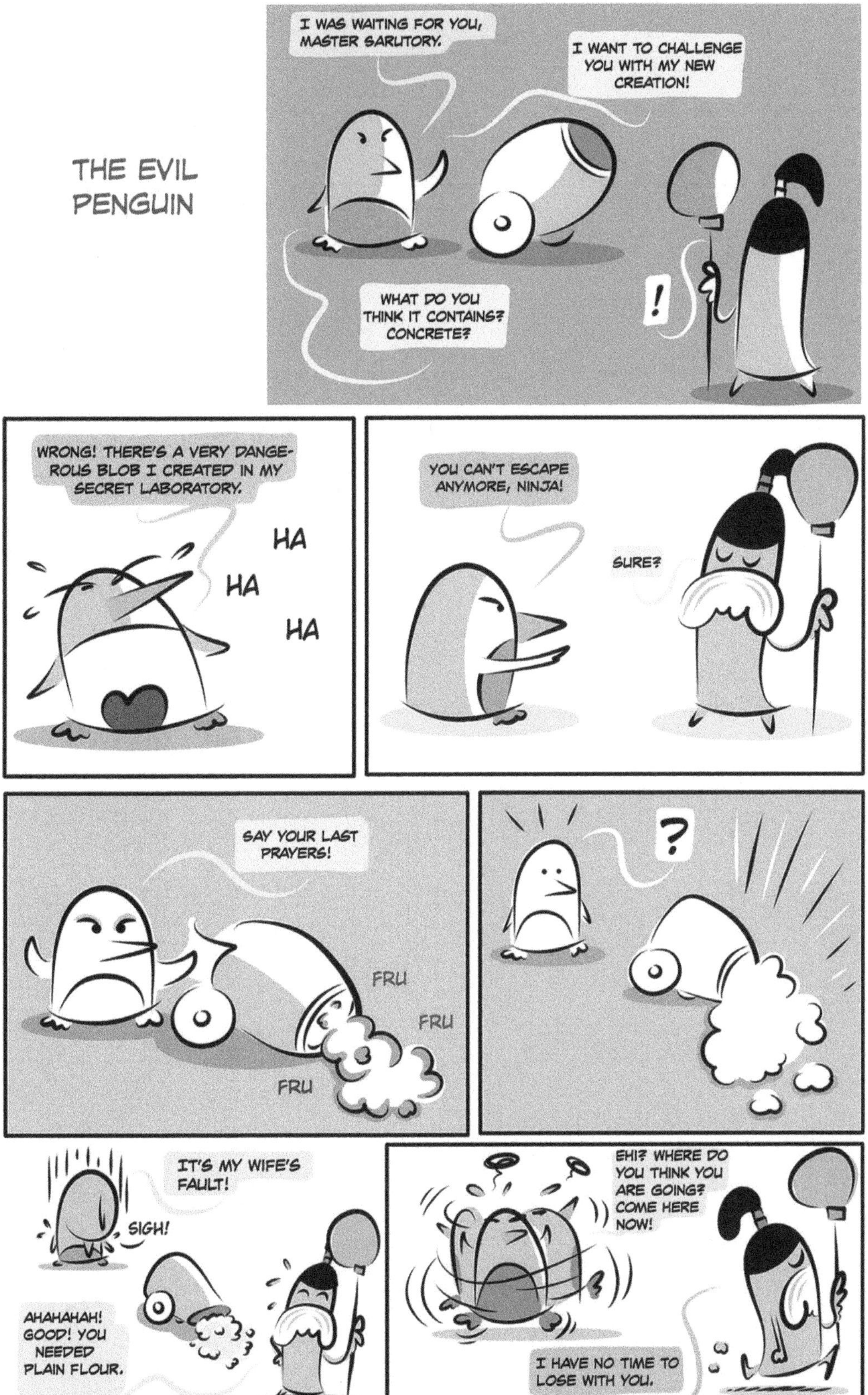

I WAS WAITING FOR YOU, MASTER SARUTORY.
I WANT TO CHALLENGE YOU WITH MY NEW CREATION!
WHAT DO YOU THINK IT CONTAINS? CONCRETE?
!
WRONG! THERE'S A VERY DANGEROUS BLOB I CREATED IN MY SECRET LABORATORY.
HA
HA
HA
YOU CAN'T ESCAPE ANYMORE, NINJA!
SURE?
SAY YOUR LAST PRAYERS!
FRU
FRU
FRU
?
IT'S MY WIFE'S FAULT!
SIGH!
AHAHAHAH! GOOD! YOU NEEDED PLAIN FLOUR.
EHI? WHERE DO YOU THINK YOU ARE GOING? COME HERE NOW!
I HAVE NO TIME TO LOSE WITH YOU.

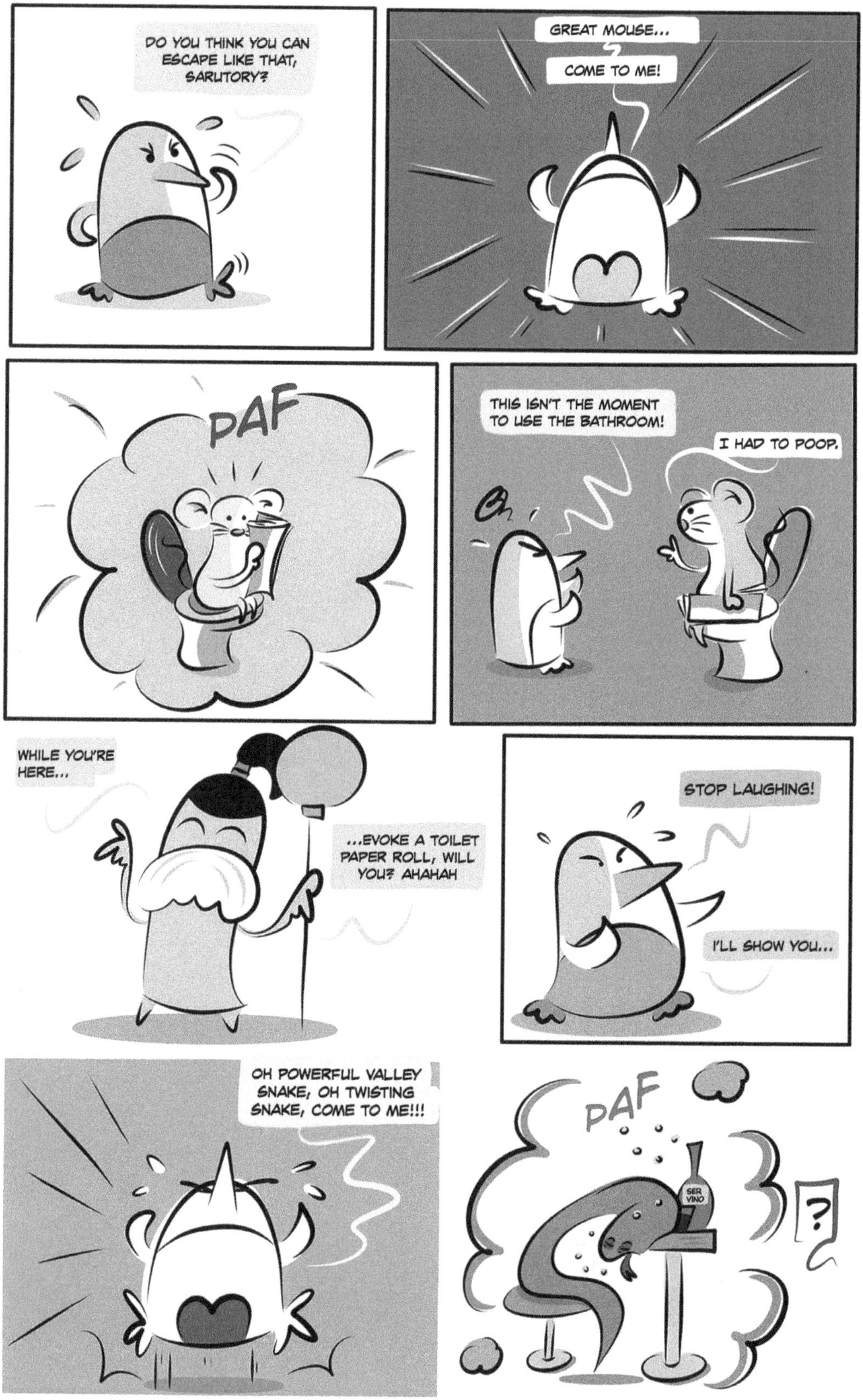
DO YOU THINK YOU CAN ESCAPE LIKE THAT, SARUTORY?
GREAT MOUSE...
COME TO ME!
PAF
THIS ISN'T THE MOMENT TO USE THE BATHROOM!
I HAD TO POOP.
WHILE YOU'RE HERE...
...EVOKE A TOILET PAPER ROLL, WILL YOU? AHAHAH
STOP LAUGHING!
I'LL SHOW YOU...
OH POWERFUL VALLEY SNAKE, OH TWISTING SNAKE, COME TO ME!!!
PAF
SER VINO
?

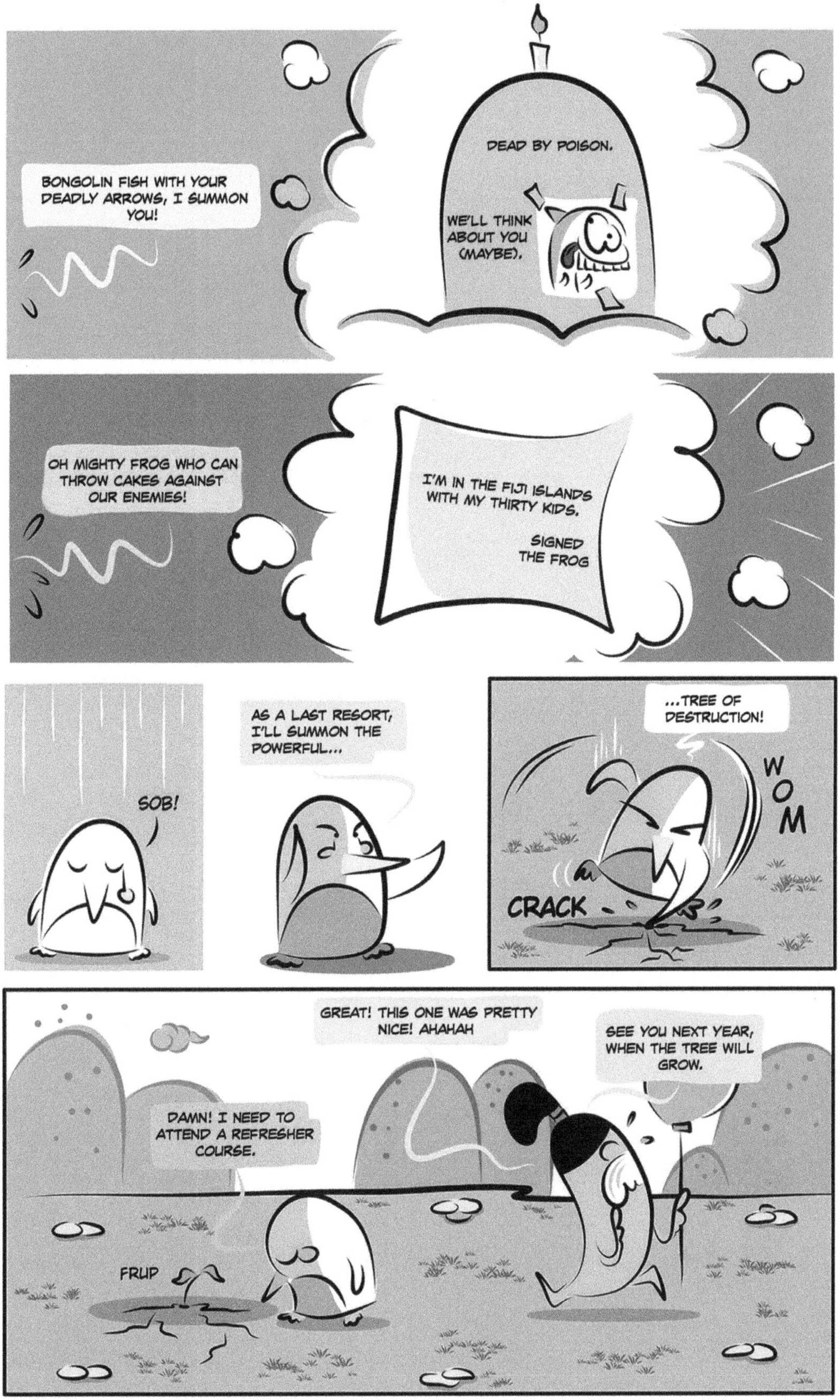
BONGOLIN FISH WITH YOUR DEADLY ARROWS, I SUMMON YOU!
DEAD BY POISON.
WE'LL THINK ABOUT YOU (MAYBE).
OH MIGHTY FROG WHO CAN THROW CAKES AGAINST OUR ENEMIES!
I'M IN THE FIJI ISLANDS WITH MY THIRTY KIDS.
SIGNED THE FROG
SOB!
AS A LAST RESORT, I'LL SUMMON THE POWERFUL...
...TREE OF DESTRUCTION!
WOM
CRACK
GREAT! THIS ONE WAS PRETTY NICE! AHAHAH
SEE YOU NEXT YEAR, WHEN THE TREE WILL GROW.
DAMN! I NEED TO ATTEND A REFRESHER COURSE.
FRUP

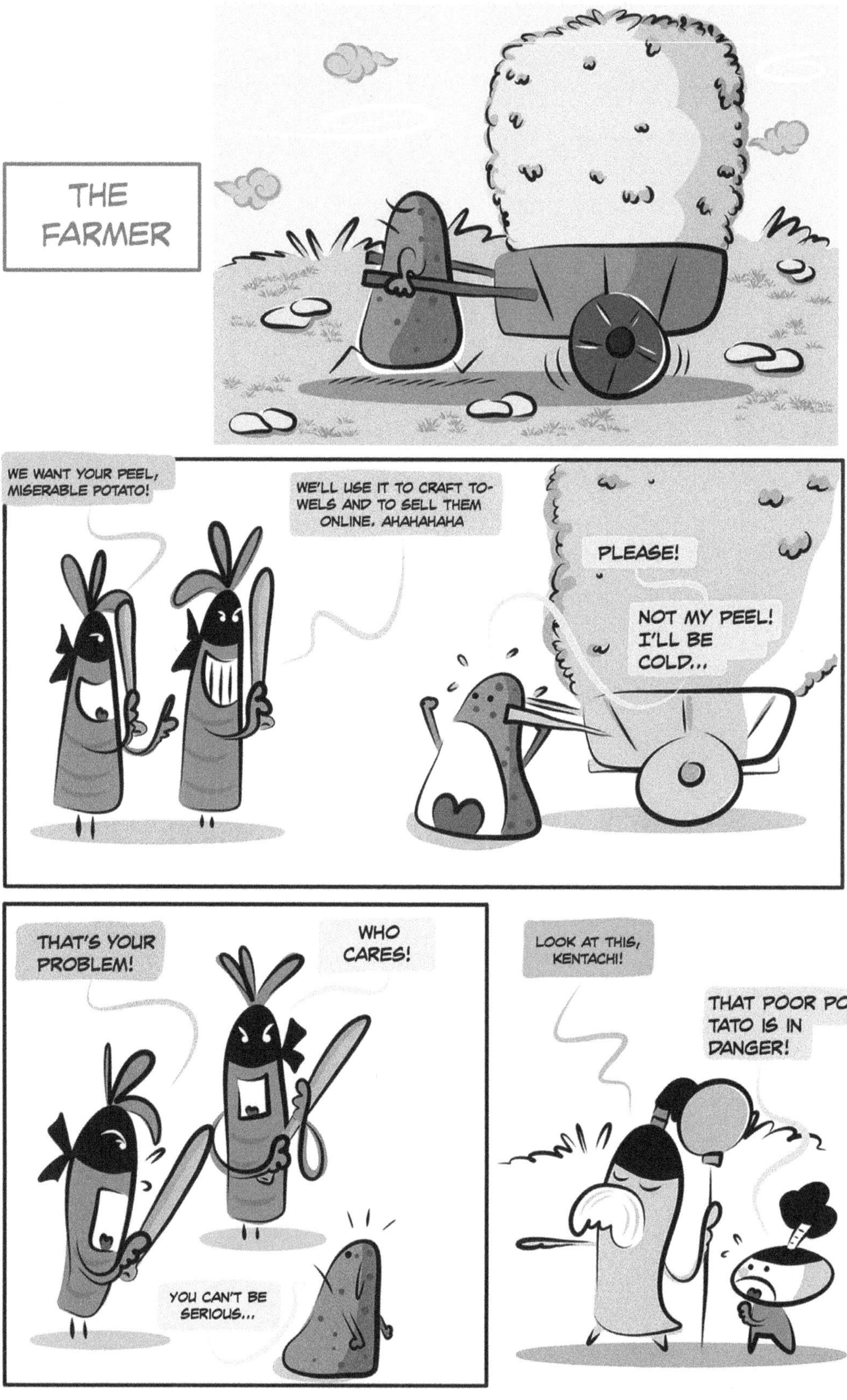
THE FARMER
WE WANT YOUR PEEL, MISERABLE POTATO!
WE'LL USE IT TO CRAFT TO-WELS AND TO SELL THEM ONLINE. AHAHAHAHA
PLEASE!
NOT MY PEEL! I'LL BE COLD...
THAT'S YOUR PROBLEM!
WHO CARES!
YOU CAN'T BE SERIOUS...
LOOK AT THIS, KENTACHI!
THAT POOR PO-TATO IS IN DANGER!

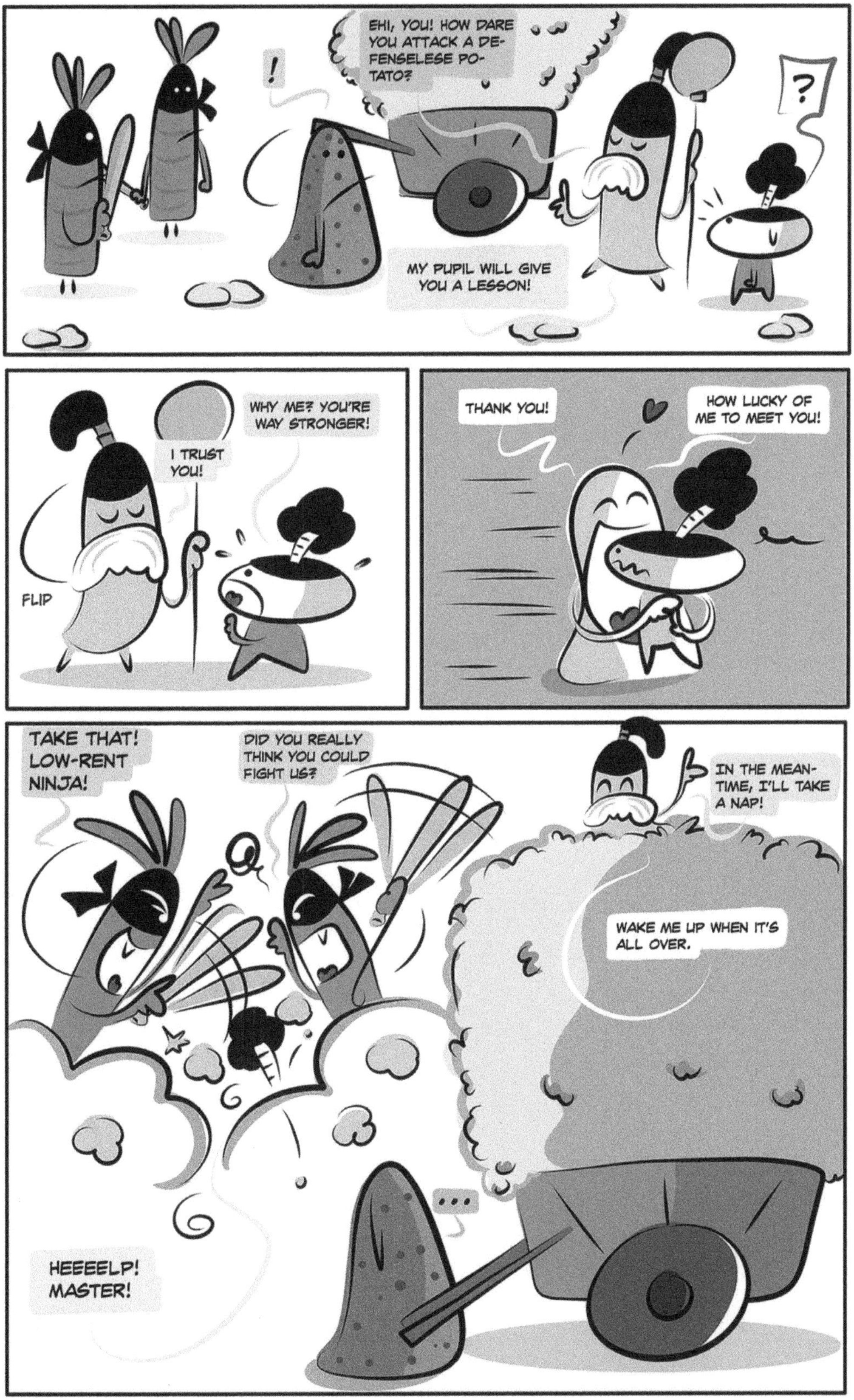
!
EHI, YOU! HOW DARE YOU ATTACK A DEFENSELESE POTATO?
?
MY PUPIL WILL GIVE YOU A LESSON!
I TRUST YOU!
WHY ME? YOU'RE WAY STRONGER!
FLIP
THANK YOU!
HOW LUCKY OF ME TO MEET YOU!
TAKE THAT! LOW-RENT NINJA!
DID YOU REALLY THINK YOU COULD FIGHT US?
IN THE MEAN-TIME, I'LL TAKE A NAP!
WAKE ME UP WHEN IT'S ALL OVER.
...
HEEEELP! MASTER!

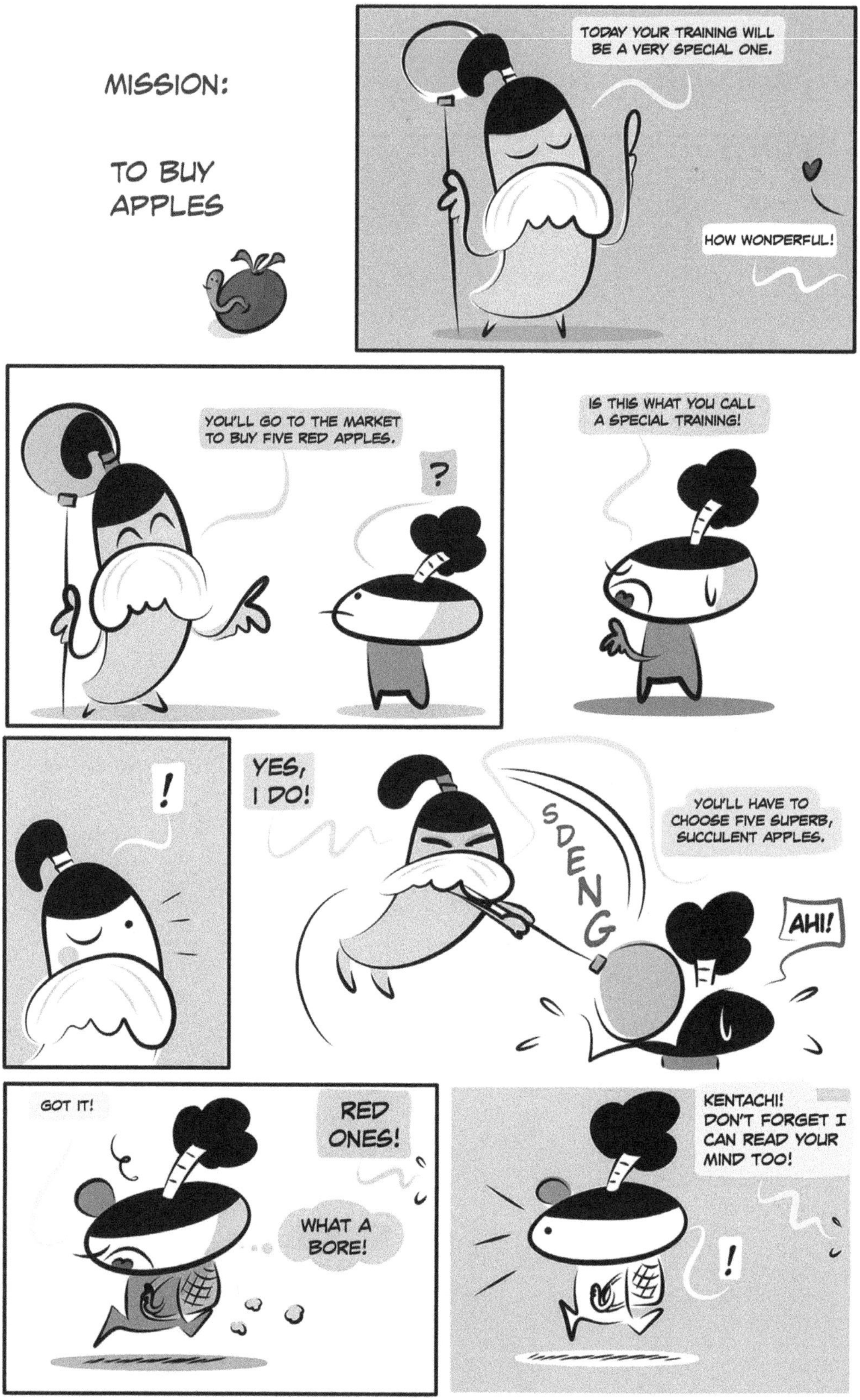
MISSION:
TO BUY APPLES
TODAY YOUR TRAINING WILL BE A VERY SPECIAL ONE.
HOW WONDERFUL!
YOU'LL GO TO THE MARKET TO BUY FIVE RED APPLES.
?
IS THIS WHAT YOU CALL A SPECIAL TRAINING!
!
YES, I DO!
SDENG
YOU'LL HAVE TO CHOOSE FIVE SUPERB, SUCCULENT APPLES.
AHI!
GOT IT!
RED ONES!
WHAT A BORE!
KENTACHI! DON'T FORGET I CAN READ YOUR MIND TOO!
!

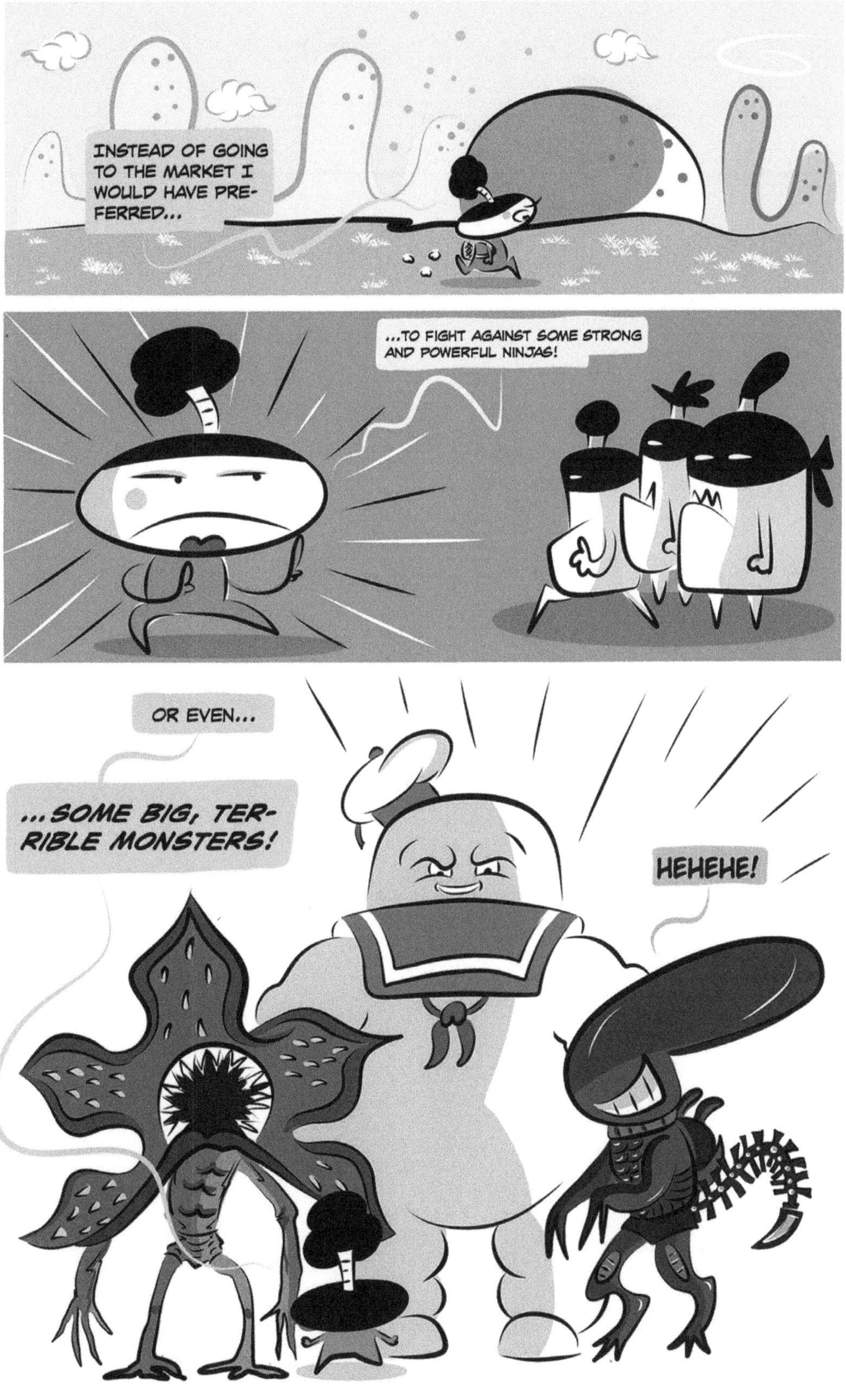
INSTEAD OF GOING TO THE MARKET I WOULD HAVE PRE- FERRED...
...TO FIGHT AGAINST SOME STRONG AND POWERFUL NINJAS!
OR EVEN...
...SOME BIG, TER- RIBLE MONSTERS!
HEHEHE!

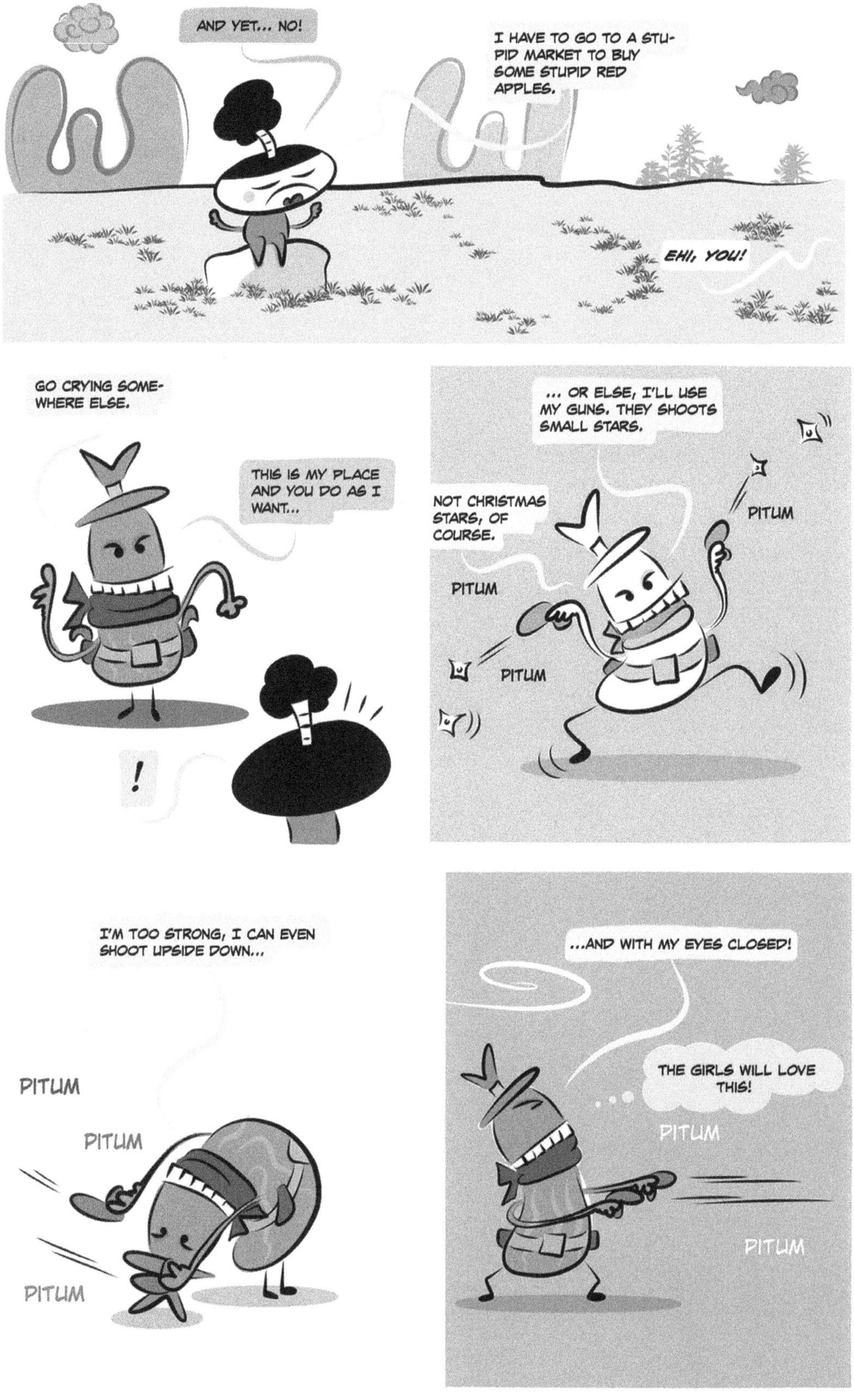
AND YET... NO!
I HAVE TO GO TO A STU-PID MARKET TO BUY SOME STUPID RED APPLES.
EHI, YOU!
GO CRYING SOME-WHERE ELSE.
THIS IS MY PLACE AND YOU DO AS I WANT...
!
... OR ELSE, I'LL USE MY GUNS. THEY SHOOTS SMALL STARS.
NOT CHRISTMAS STARS, OF COURSE.
PITUM
PITUM
PITUM
I'M TOO STRONG, I CAN EVEN SHOOT UPSIDE DOWN...
PITUM
PITUM
PITUM
...AND WITH MY EYES CLOSED!
THE GIRLS WILL LOVE THIS!
PITUM
PITUM

LOOK HOW I HIT THIS HUGE ROCK...
FUM
FUM
FUM
ROLL
ROLL
ROLL
YEP, YOU'RE REALLY GOOD WITH YOUR GUNS.
BUT I HAVE TO GO NOW, I HAVE A VERY IMPORTANT TASK TO DO.
HELLO! DO YOU HA-VE SUPERB, SUCCU-LENT APPLES?
NO, SORRY. BUT I HAVE VERY GOOD RED BERRIES.
NEVERMIND.
I'LL TELL MASTER THAT IT'S TOO HOT TO FIND SUPERB, SUCCULENT APPLES.

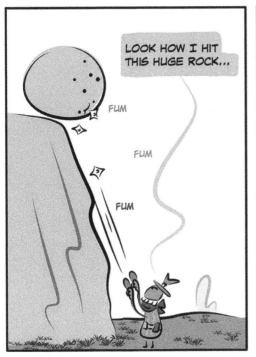

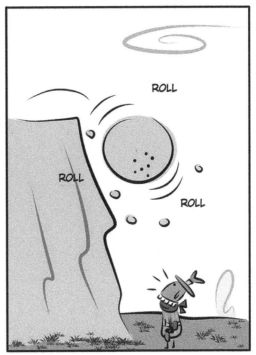

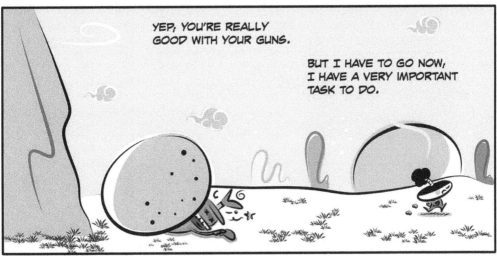

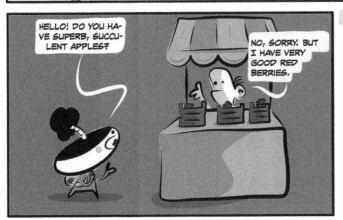

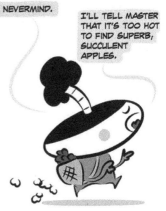

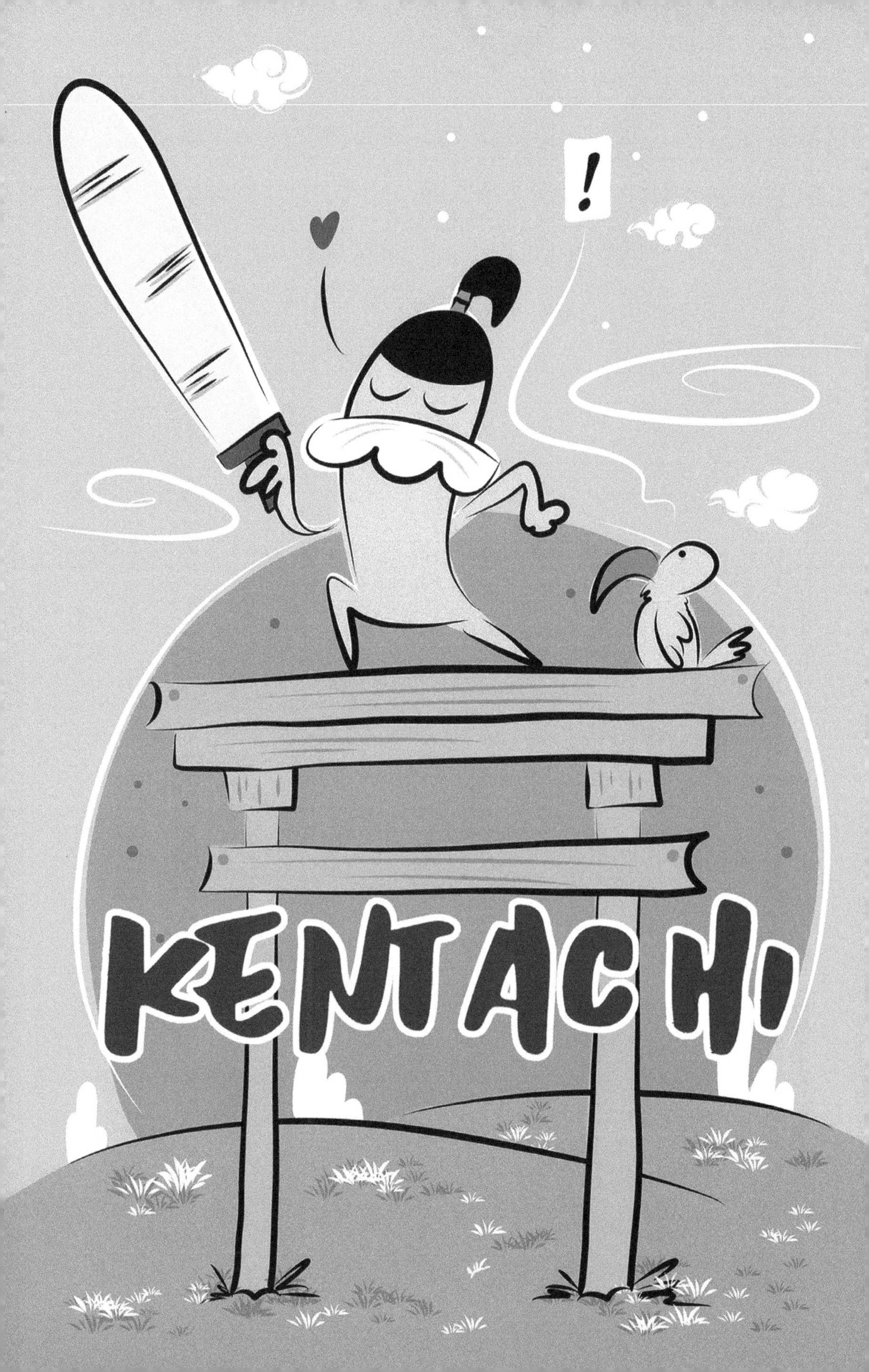
!
KENTACHI

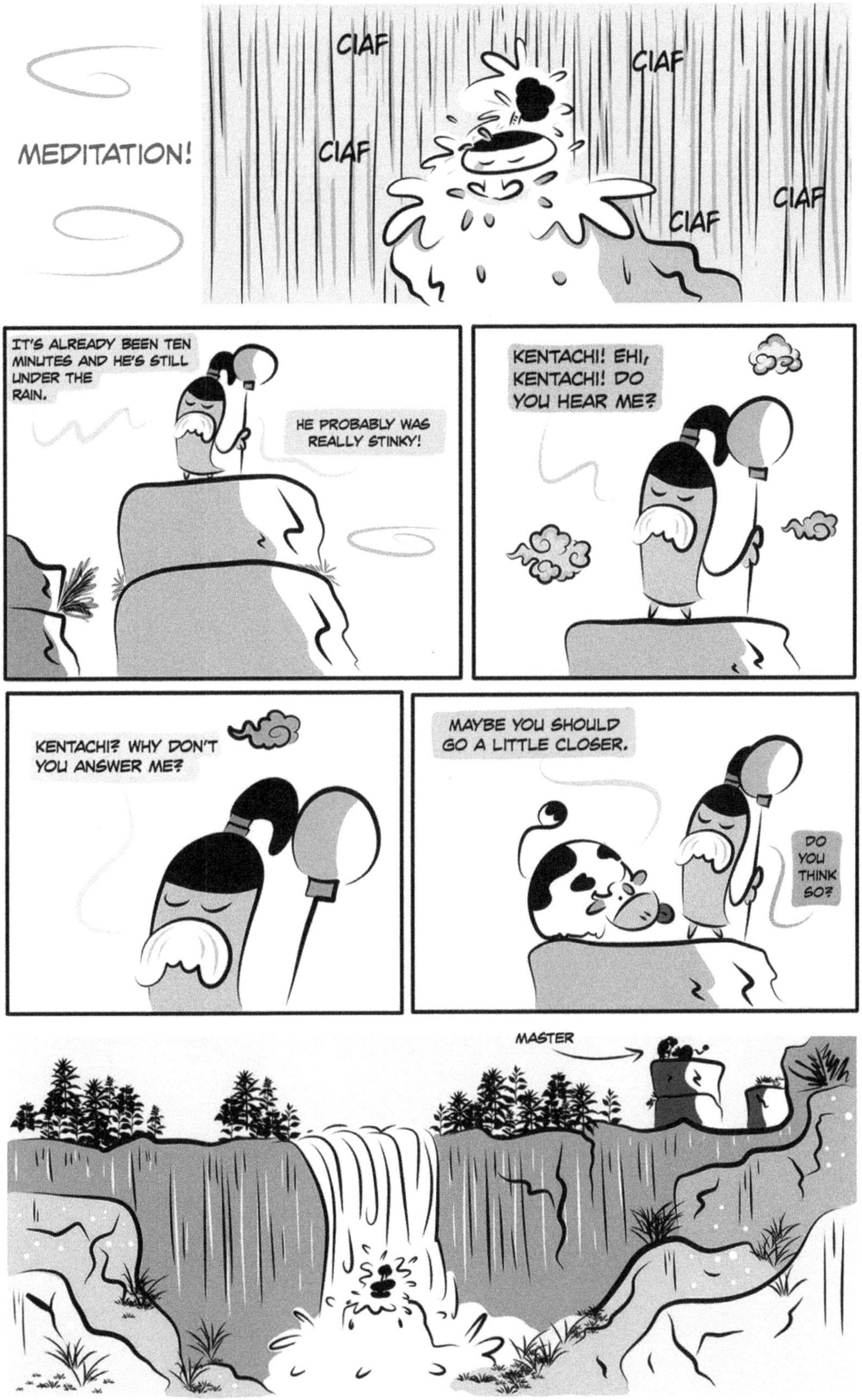
MEDITATION!
CIAF
CIAF
CIAF
CIAF
CIAF
IT'S ALREADY BEEN TEN MINUTES AND HE'S STILL UNDER THE RAIN.
HE PROBABLY WAS REALLY STINKY!
KENTACHI! EHI, KENTACHI! DO YOU HEAR ME?
KENTACHI? WHY DON'T YOU ANSWER ME?
MAYBE YOU SHOULD GO A LITTLE CLOSER.
DO YOU THINK SO?
MASTER

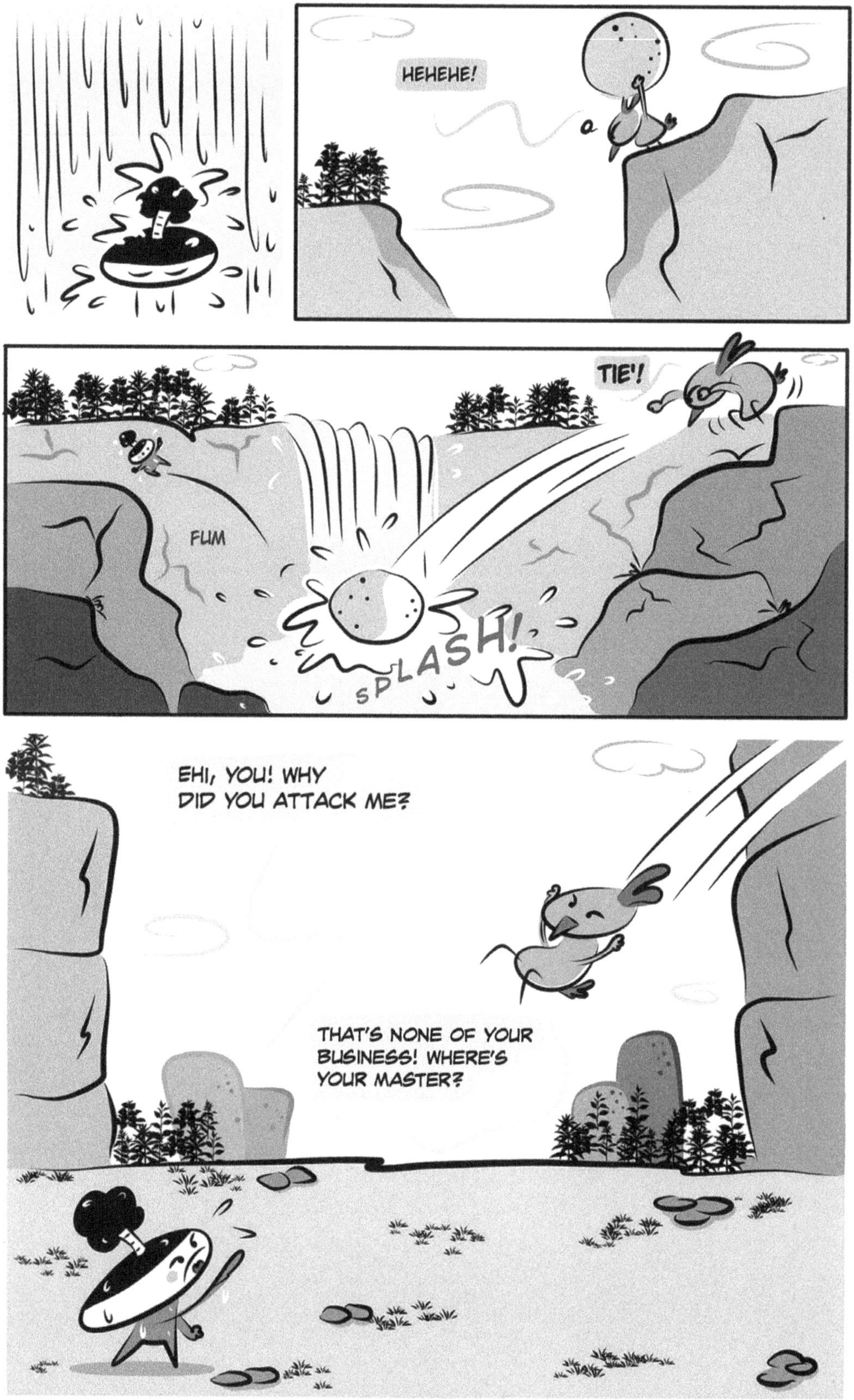
HEHEHE!
TIE'!
FUM
SPLASH!
EHI, YOU! WHY DID YOU ATTACK ME?
THAT'S NONE OF YOUR BUSINESS! WHERE'S YOUR MASTER?

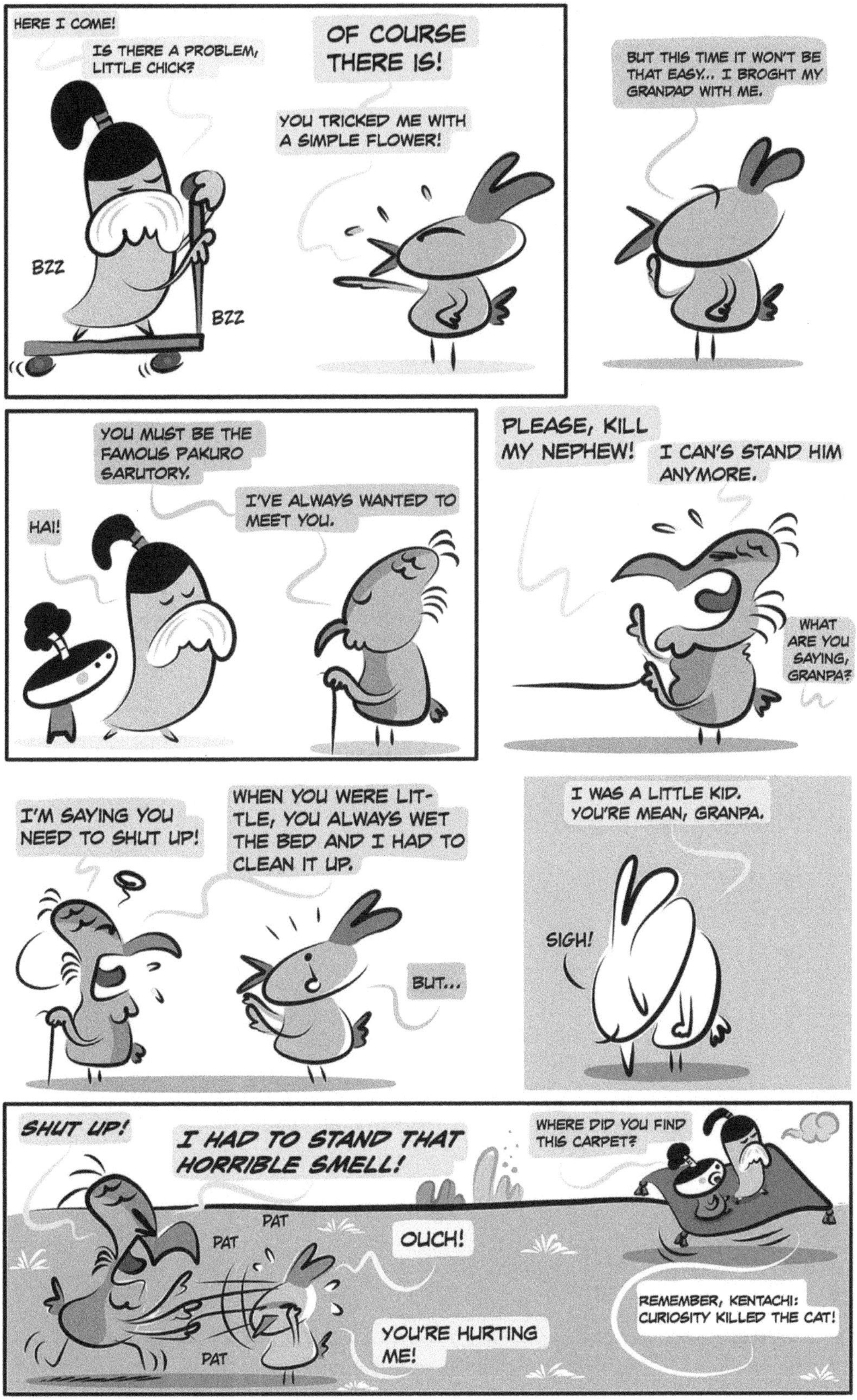
HERE I COME!
IS THERE A PROBLEM, LITTLE CHICK?
OF COURSE THERE IS!
YOU TRICKED ME WITH A SIMPLE FLOWER!
BZZ
BZZ
BUT THIS TIME IT WON'T BE THAT EASY... I BROGHT MY GRANDAD WITH ME.
YOU MUST BE THE FAMOUS PAKURO SARUTORY.
HAI!
I'VE ALWAYS WANTED TO MEET YOU.
PLEASE, KILL MY NEPHEW!
I CAN'S STAND HIM ANYMORE.
WHAT ARE YOU SAYING, GRANPA?
I'M SAYING YOU NEED TO SHUT UP!
WHEN YOU WERE LIT-TLE, YOU ALWAYS WET THE BED AND I HAD TO CLEAN IT UP.
BUT...
I WAS A LITTLE KID. YOU'RE MEAN, GRANPA.
SIGH!
SHUT UP!
I HAD TO STAND THAT HORRIBLE SMELL!
WHERE DID YOU FIND THIS CARPET?
PAT
PAT
OUCH!
PAT
YOU'RE HURTING ME!
REMEMBER, KENTACHI: CURIOSITY KILLED THE CAT!

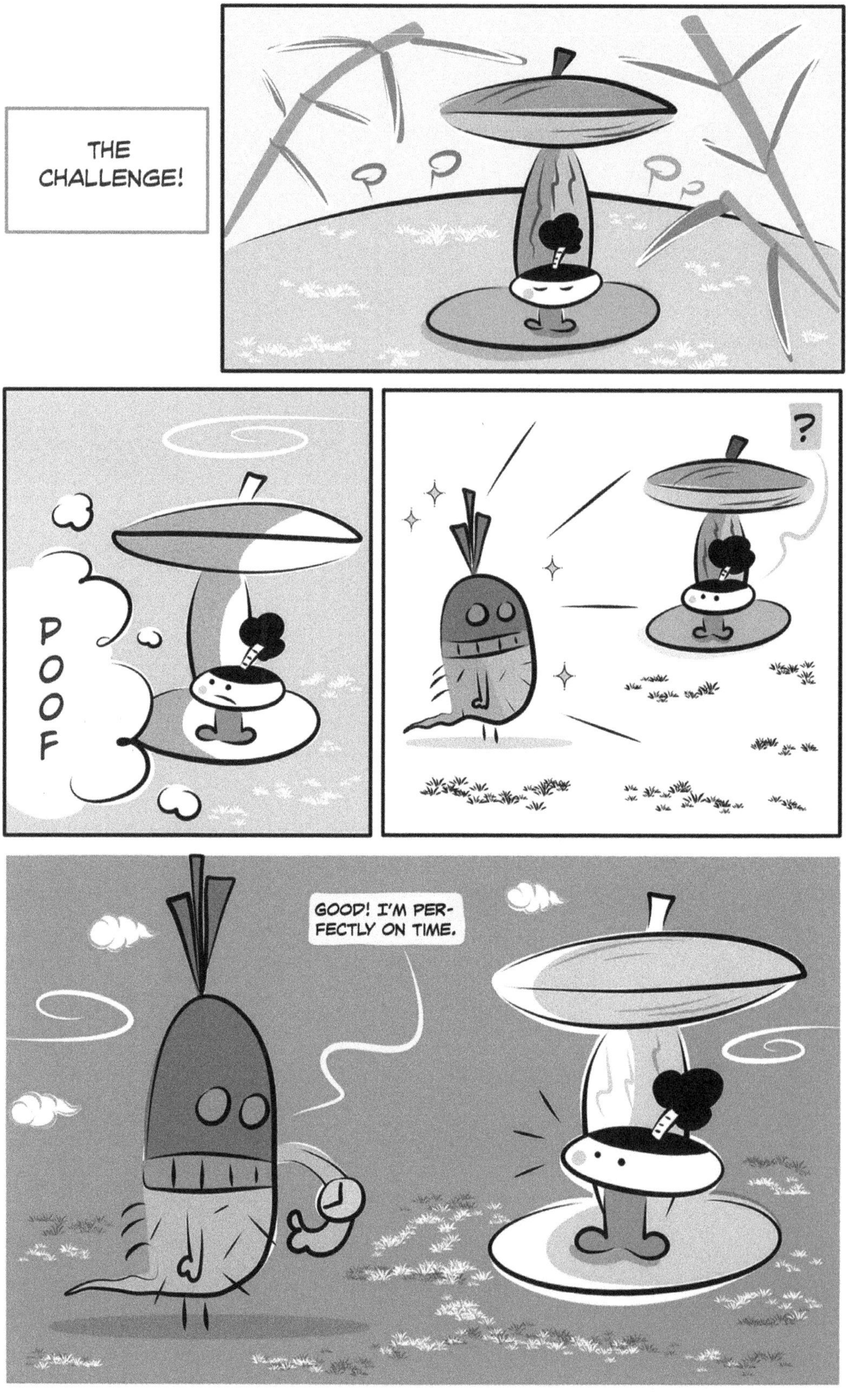
THE CHALLENGE!
POOF
?
GOOD! I'M PERFECTLY ON TIME.

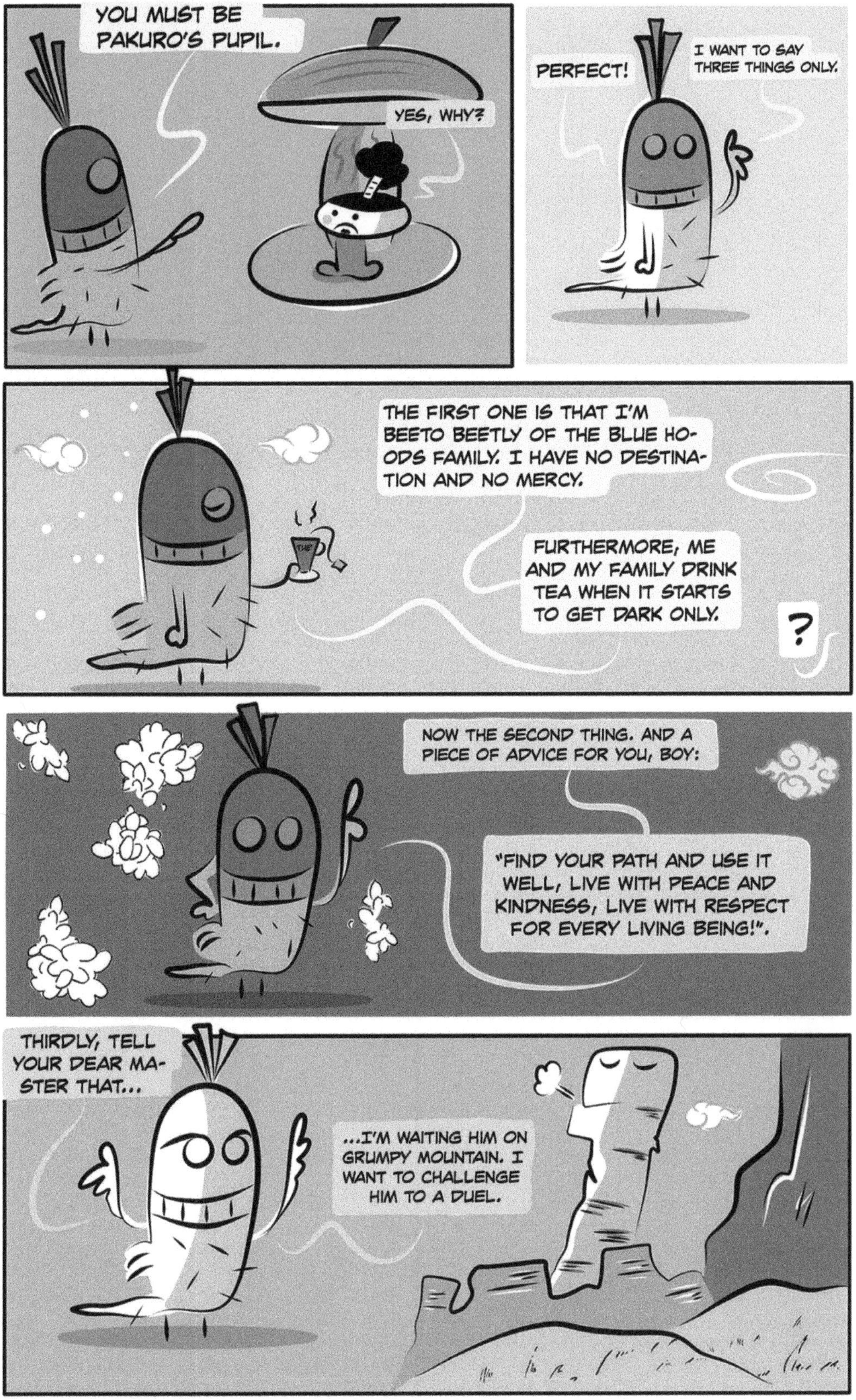
YOU MUST BE PAKURO'S PUPIL.
YES, WHY?
PERFECT!
I WANT TO SAY THREE THINGS ONLY.
THE FIRST ONE IS THAT I'M BEETO BEETLY OF THE BLUE HO-ODS FAMILY. I HAVE NO DESTINA-TION AND NO MERCY.
THE
FURTHERMORE, ME AND MY FAMILY DRINK TEA WHEN IT STARTS TO GET DARK ONLY.
?
NOW THE SECOND THING. AND A PIECE OF ADVICE FOR YOU, BOY:
"FIND YOUR PATH AND USE IT WELL, LIVE WITH PEACE AND KINDNESS, LIVE WITH RESPECT FOR EVERY LIVING BEING!".
THIRDLY, TELL YOUR DEAR MA-STER THAT...
...I'M WAITING HIM ON GRUMPY MOUNTAIN. I WANT TO CHALLENGE HIM TO A DUEL.

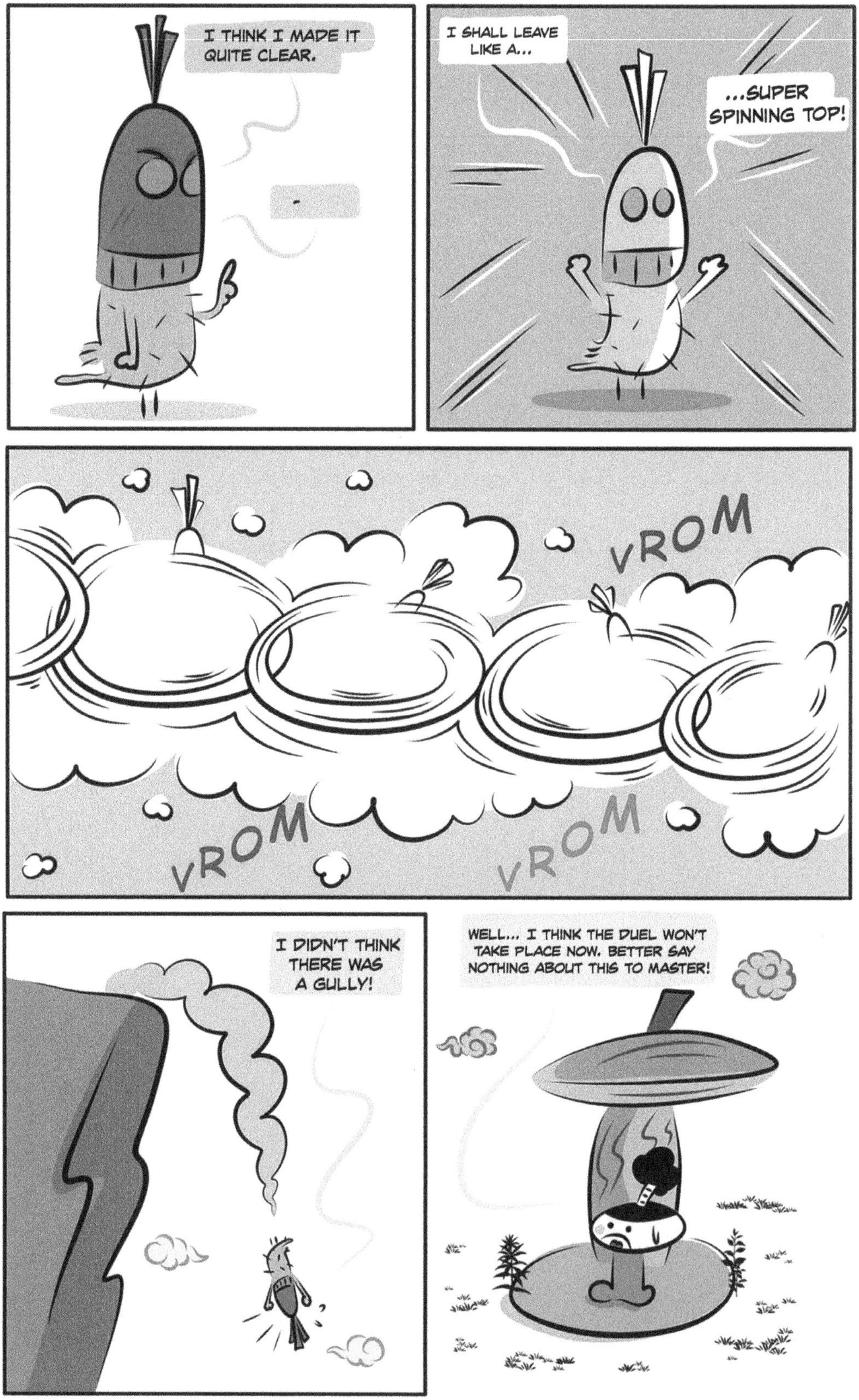
I THINK I MADE IT QUITE CLEAR.
-
I SHALL LEAVE LIKE A...
...SUPER SPINNING TOP!
VROM
VROM
VROM
I DIDN'T THINK THERE WAS A GULLY!
WELL... I THINK THE DUEL WON'T TAKE PLACE NOW. BETTER SAY NOTHING ABOUT THIS TO MASTER!

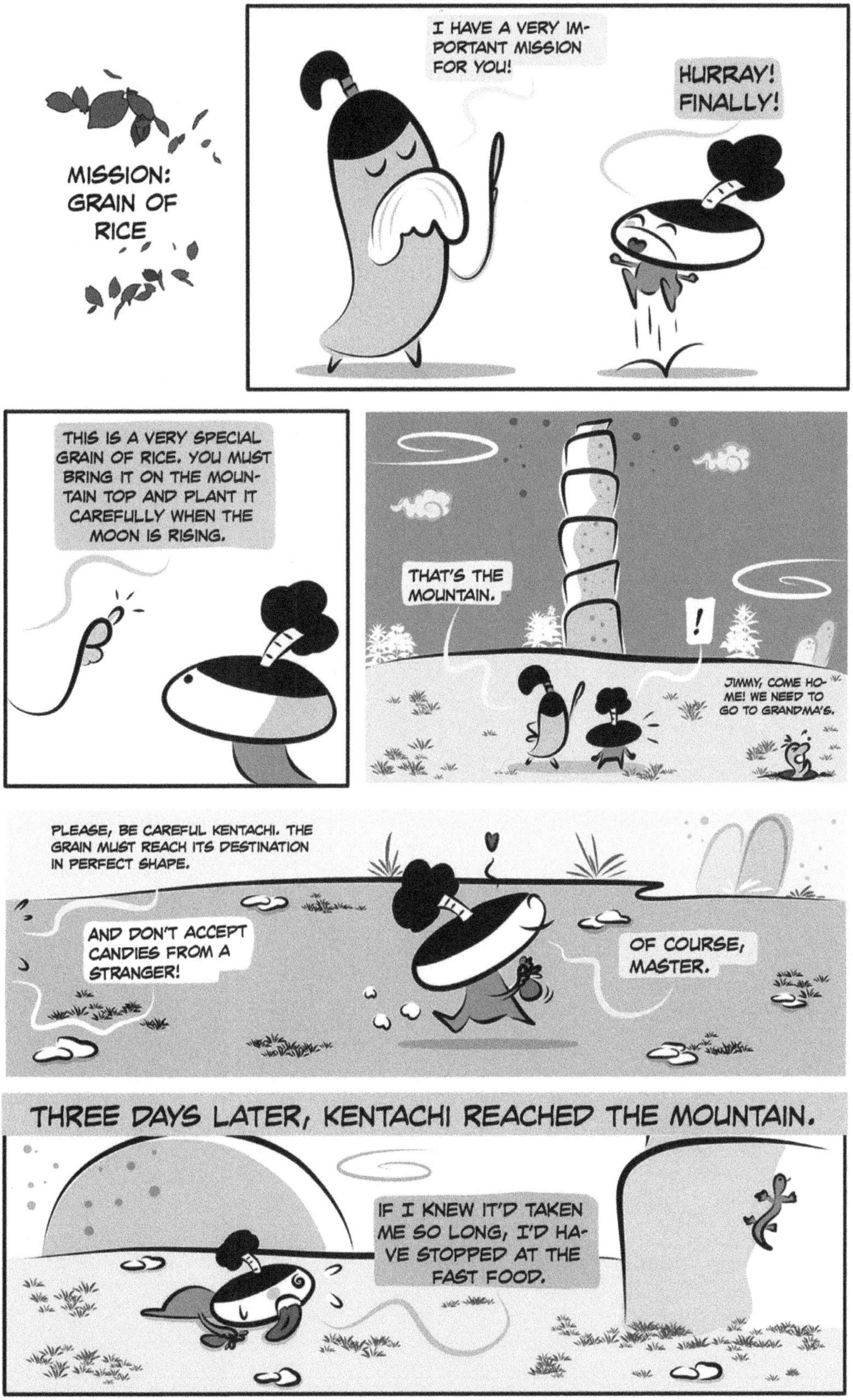
MISSION: GRAIN OF RICE
I HAVE A VERY IM-PORTANT MISSION FOR YOU!
HURRAY! FINALLY!
THIS IS A VERY SPECIAL GRAIN OF RICE. YOU MUST BRING IT ON THE MOUN-TAIN TOP AND PLANT IT CAREFULLY WHEN THE MOON IS RISING.
THAT'S THE MOUNTAIN.
!
JIMMY, COME HO-ME! WE NEED TO GO TO GRANDMA'S.
PLEASE, BE CAREFUL KENTACHI. THE GRAIN MUST REACH ITS DESTINATION IN PERFECT SHAPE.
AND DON'T ACCEPT CANDIES FROM A STRANGER!
OF COURSE, MASTER.
THREE DAYS LATER, KENTACHI REACHED THE MOUNTAIN.
IF I KNEW IT'D TAKEN ME SO LONG, I'D HA-VE STOPPED AT THE FAST FOOD.

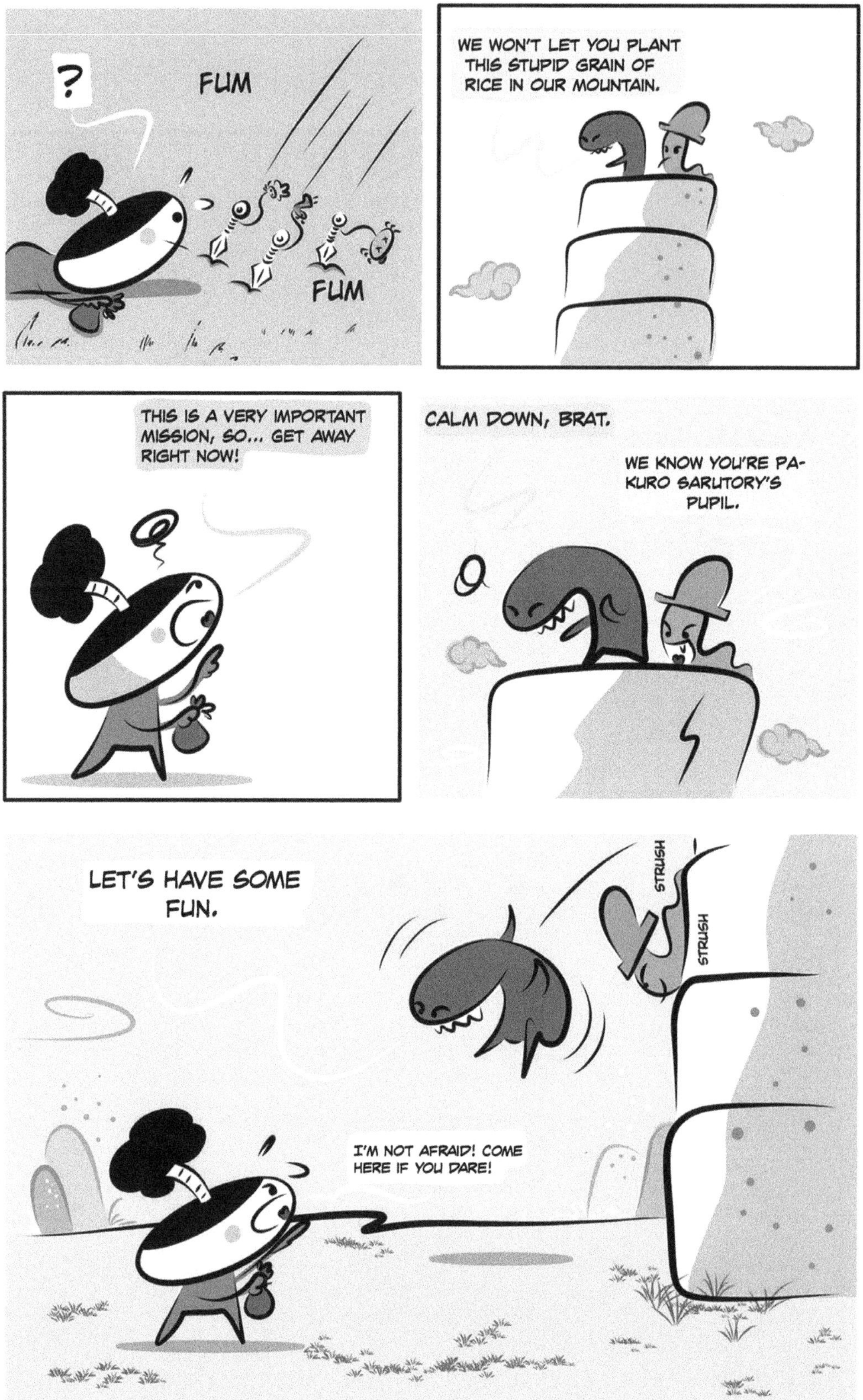
?
FUM
FUM
WE WON'T LET YOU PLANT THIS STUPID GRAIN OF RICE IN OUR MOUNTAIN.
THIS IS A VERY IMPORTANT MISSION, SO... GET AWAY RIGHT NOW!
CALM DOWN, BRAT.
WE KNOW YOU'RE PA-KURO SARUTORY'S PUPIL.
LET'S HAVE SOME FUN.
STRUSH
STRUSH
I'M NOT AFRAID! COME HERE IF YOU DARE!

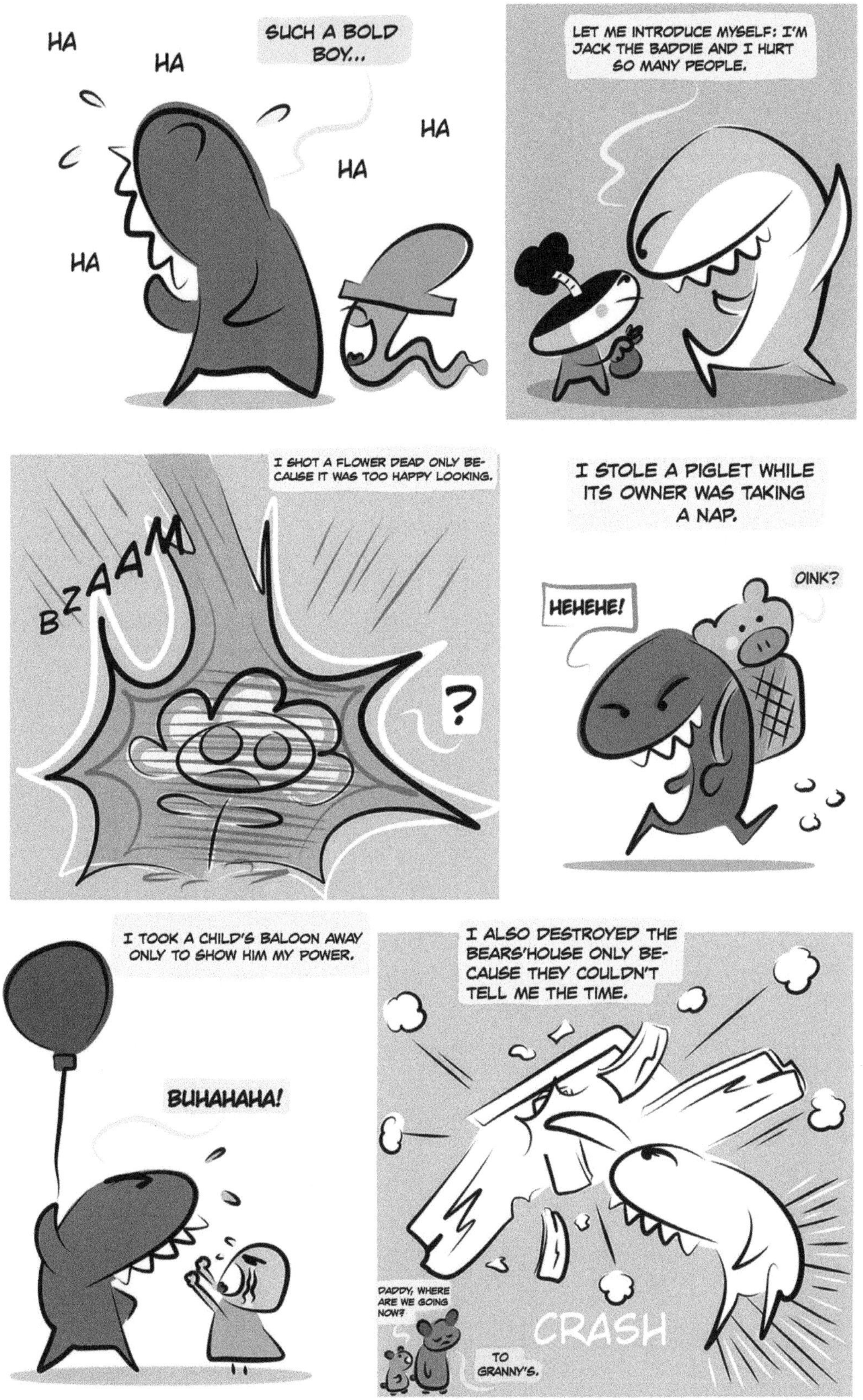

HA
HA
SUCH A BOLD BOY...
HA
HA
HA
LET ME INTRODUCE MYSELF: I'M JACK THE BADDIE AND I HURT SO MANY PEOPLE.
I SHOT A FLOWER DEAD ONLY BECAUSE IT WAS TOO HAPPY LOOKING.
BZAAAM
?
I STOLE A PIGLET WHILE ITS OWNER WAS TAKING A NAP.
OINK?
HEHEHE!
I TOOK A CHILD'S BALOON AWAY ONLY TO SHOW HIM MY POWER.
BUHAHAHA!
I ALSO DESTROYED THE BEARS'HOUSE ONLY BECAUSE THEY COULDN'T TELL ME THE TIME.
DADDY, WHERE ARE WE GOING NOW?
TO GRANNY'S.
CRASH

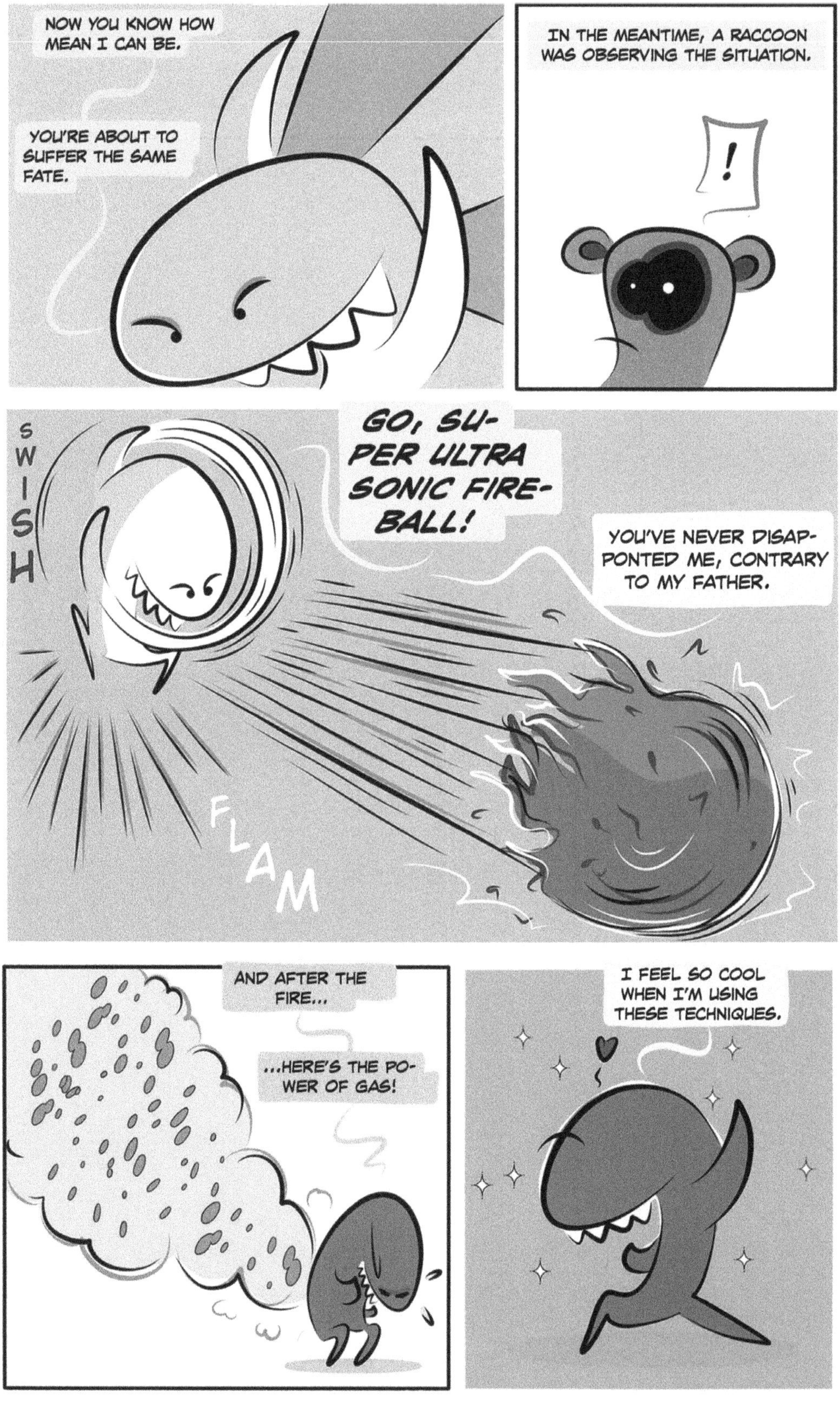
NOW YOU KNOW HOW MEAN I CAN BE.
YOU'RE ABOUT TO SUFFER THE SAME FATE.
IN THE MEANTIME, A RACCOON WAS OBSERVING THE SITUATION.
!
SWISH
GO, SU-PER ULTRA SONIC FIRE-BALL!
YOU'VE NEVER DISAP-PONTED ME, CONTRARY TO MY FATHER.
FLAM
AND AFTER THE FIRE...
...HERE'S THE PO-WER OF GAS!
I FEEL SO COOL WHEN I'M USING THESE TECHNIQUES.

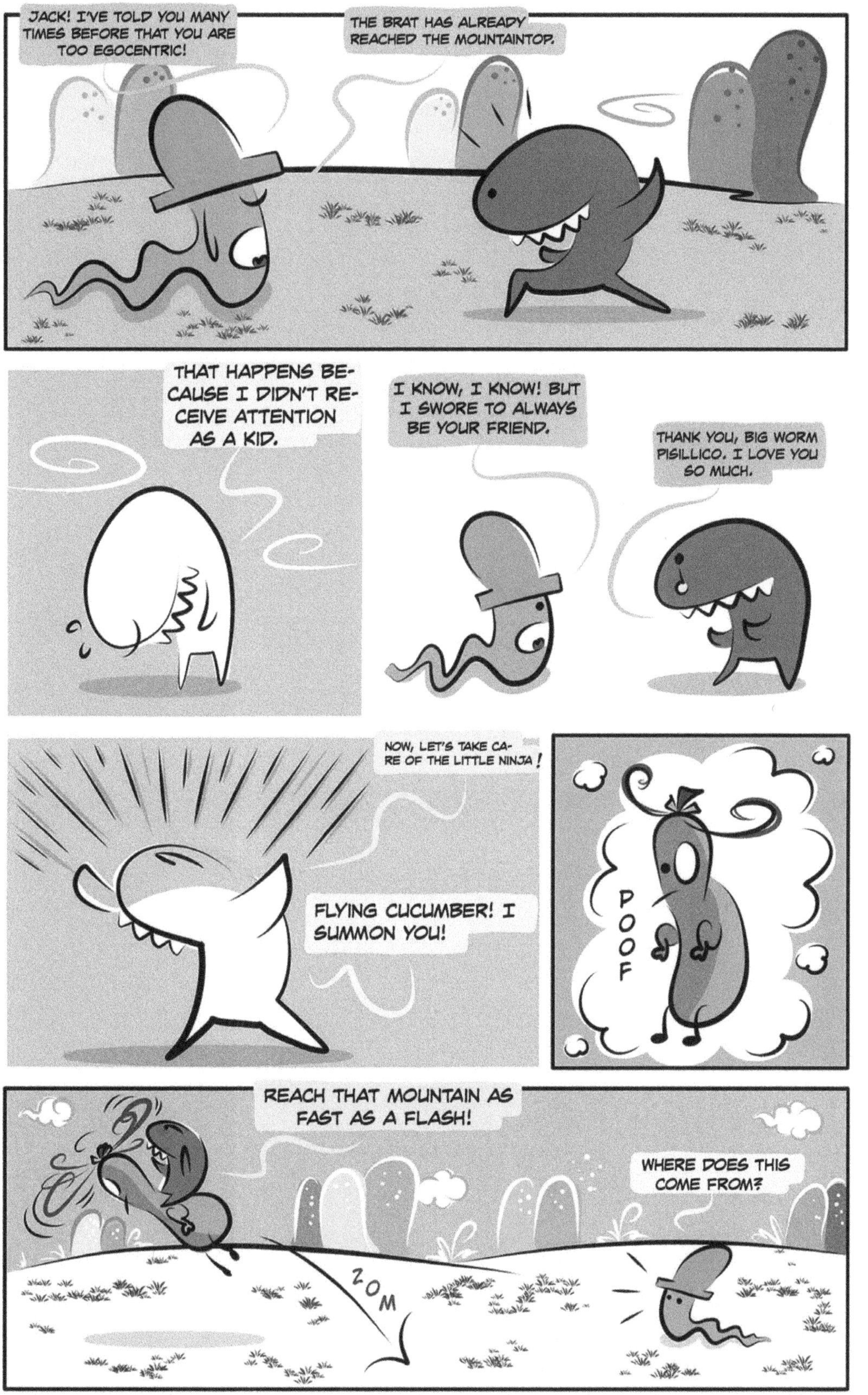
JACK! I'VE TOLD YOU MANY TIMES BEFORE THAT YOU ARE TOO EGOCENTRIC!
THE BRAT HAS ALREADY REACHED THE MOUNTAINTOP.
THAT HAPPENS BE- CAUSE I DIDN'T RE- CEIVE ATTENTION AS A KID.
I KNOW, I KNOW! BUT I SWORE TO ALWAYS BE YOUR FRIEND.
THANK YOU, BIG WORM PISILLICO. I LOVE YOU SO MUCH.
NOW, LET'S TAKE CA- RE OF THE LITTLE NINJA!
FLYING CUCUMBER! I SUMMON YOU!
POOF
REACH THAT MOUNTAIN AS FAST AS A FLASH!
ZOOM
WHERE DOES THIS COME FROM?

VICTORY IS MINE!

?

HAHAHA! YOU DUMMY!

JACK...

...THAT'S THE WRONG MOUNTAIN.

ENOUGH! IT'S TIME TO GET REAL.

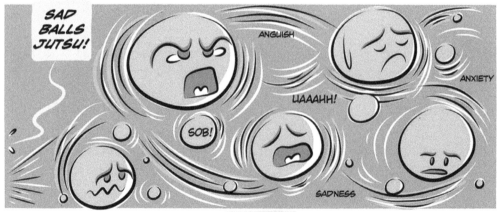

SAD BALLS JUTSU!

ANGUISH

ANXIETY

UAAAHH!

SOB!

SADNESS

NOBODY HAS EVER MANAGED TO SURVIVE!

IT'S OVER FOR YOU, BRAT.

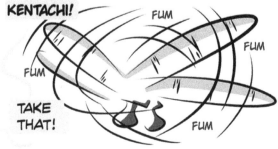

KENTACHI!

FUM

FUM

FUM

TAKE THAT!

FUM

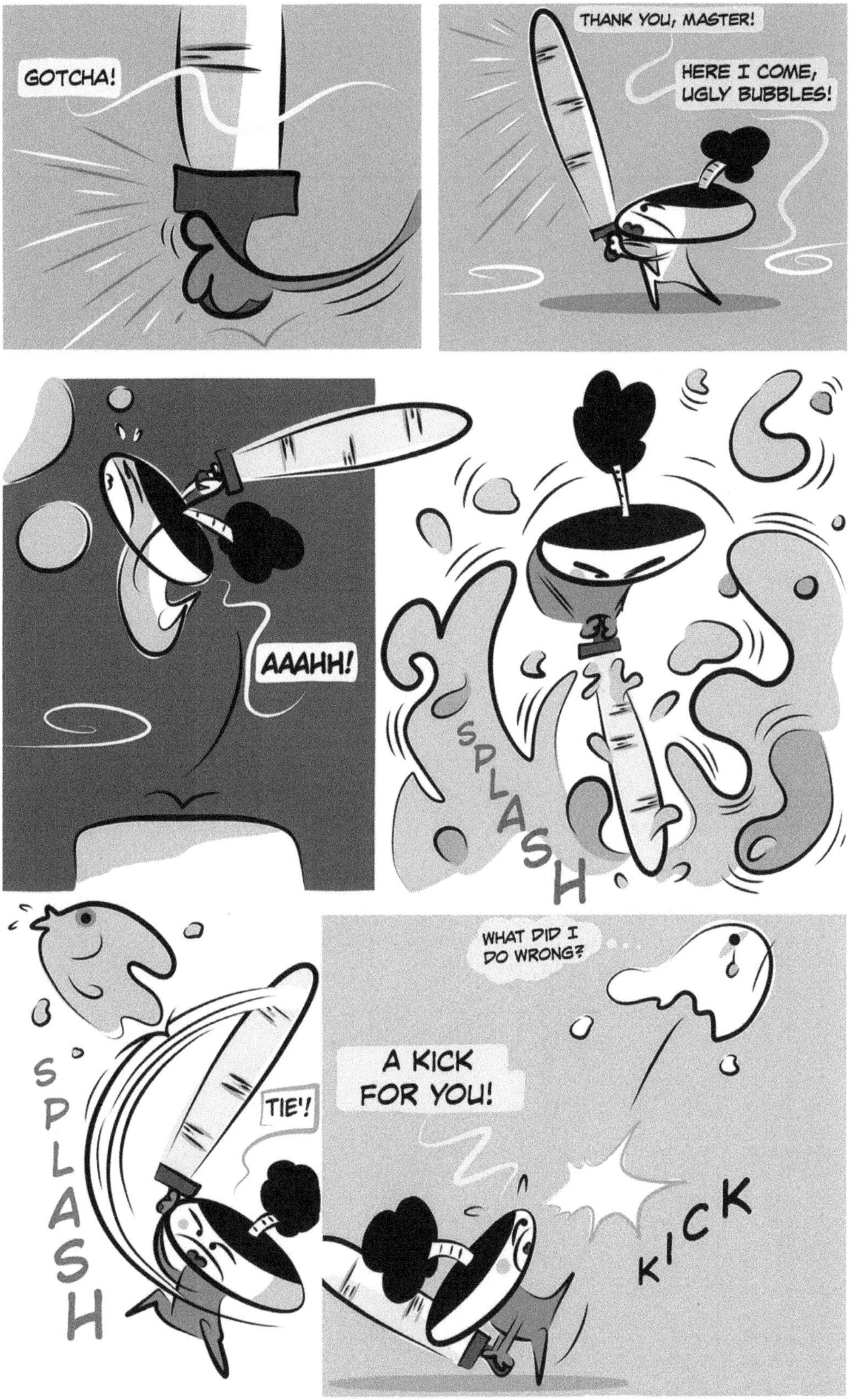
GOTCHA!
THANK YOU, MASTER!
HERE I COME, UGLY BUBBLES!
AAAHH!
SPLASH
SPLASH
TIE'!
WHAT DID I DO WRONG?
A KICK FOR YOU!
KICK

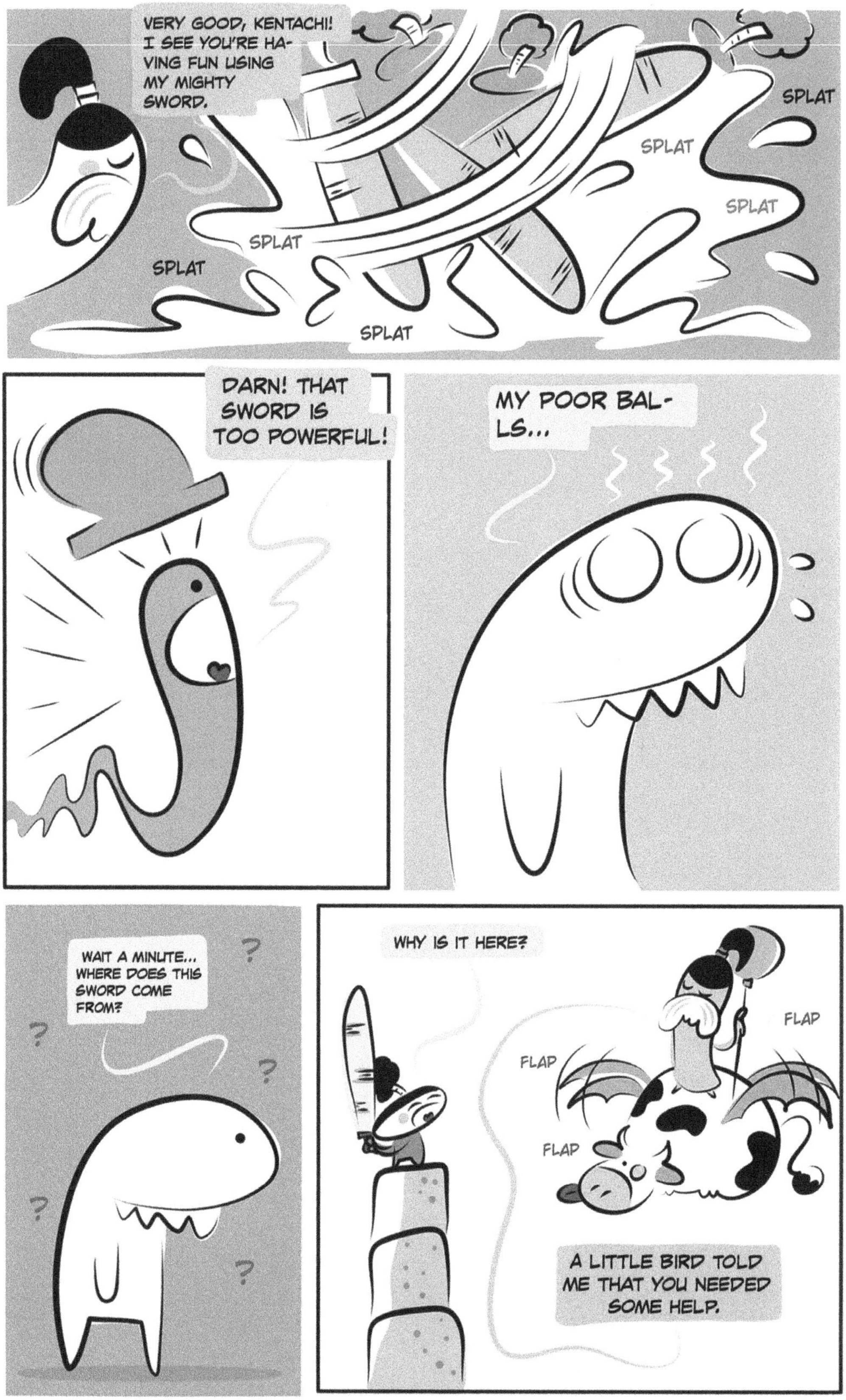
VERY GOOD, KENTACHI! I SEE YOU'RE HA-VING FUN USING MY MIGHTY SWORD.
SPLAT
SPLAT
SPLAT
SPLAT
SPLAT
SPLAT
DARN! THAT SWORD IS TOO POWERFUL!
MY POOR BAL-LS...
WAIT A MINUTE... WHERE DOES THIS SWORD COME FROM?
WHY IS IT HERE?
FLAP
FLAP
FLAP
A LITTLE BIRD TOLD ME THAT YOU NEEDED SOME HELP.

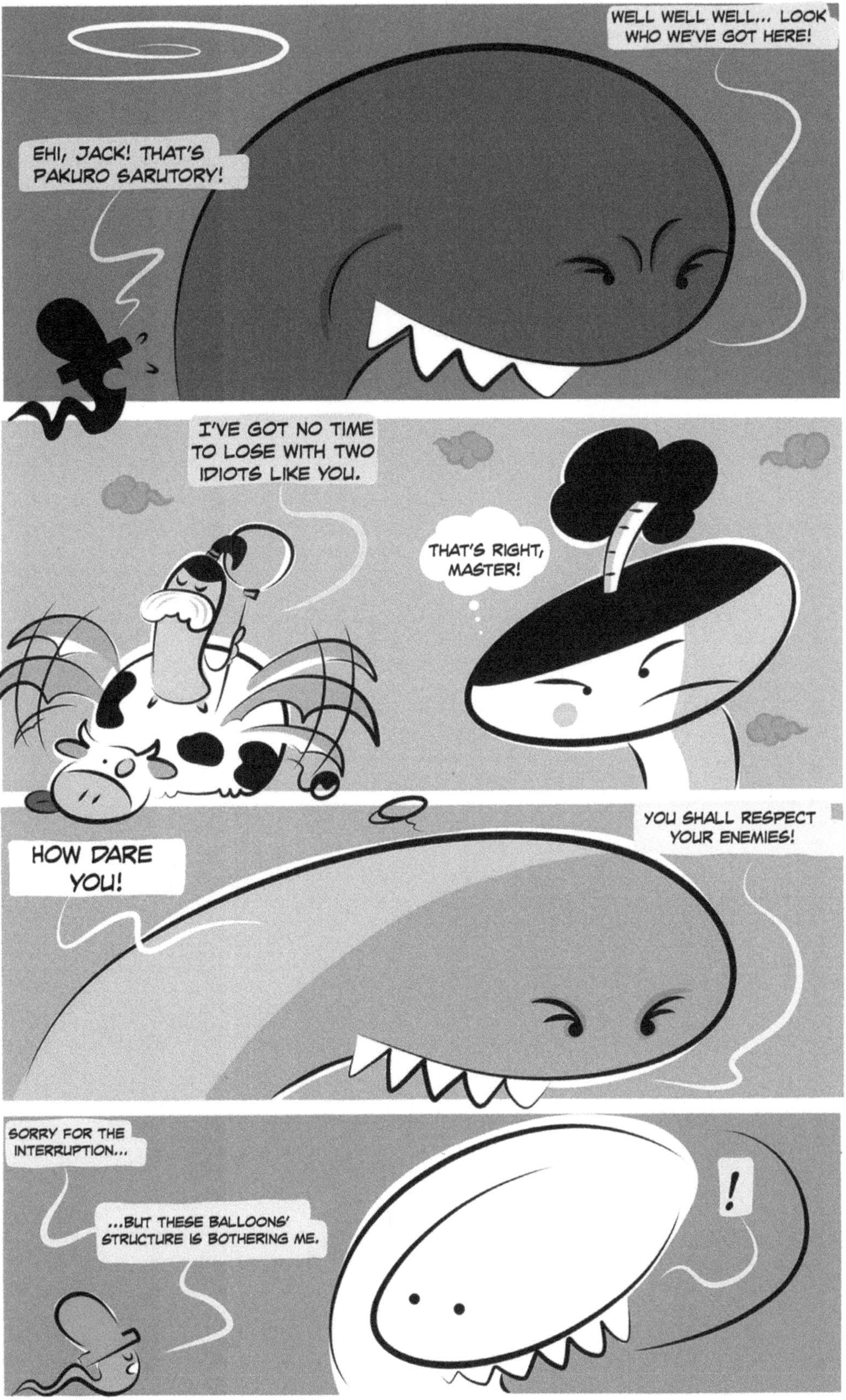
WELL WELL WELL... LOOK WHO WE'VE GOT HERE!
EHI, JACK! THAT'S PAKURO SARUTORY!
I'VE GOT NO TIME TO LOSE WITH TWO IDIOTS LIKE YOU.
THAT'S RIGHT, MASTER!
HOW DARE YOU!
YOU SHALL RESPECT YOUR ENEMIES!
SORRY FOR THE INTERRUPTION...
...BUT THESE BALLOONS' STRUCTURE IS BOTHERING ME.
!

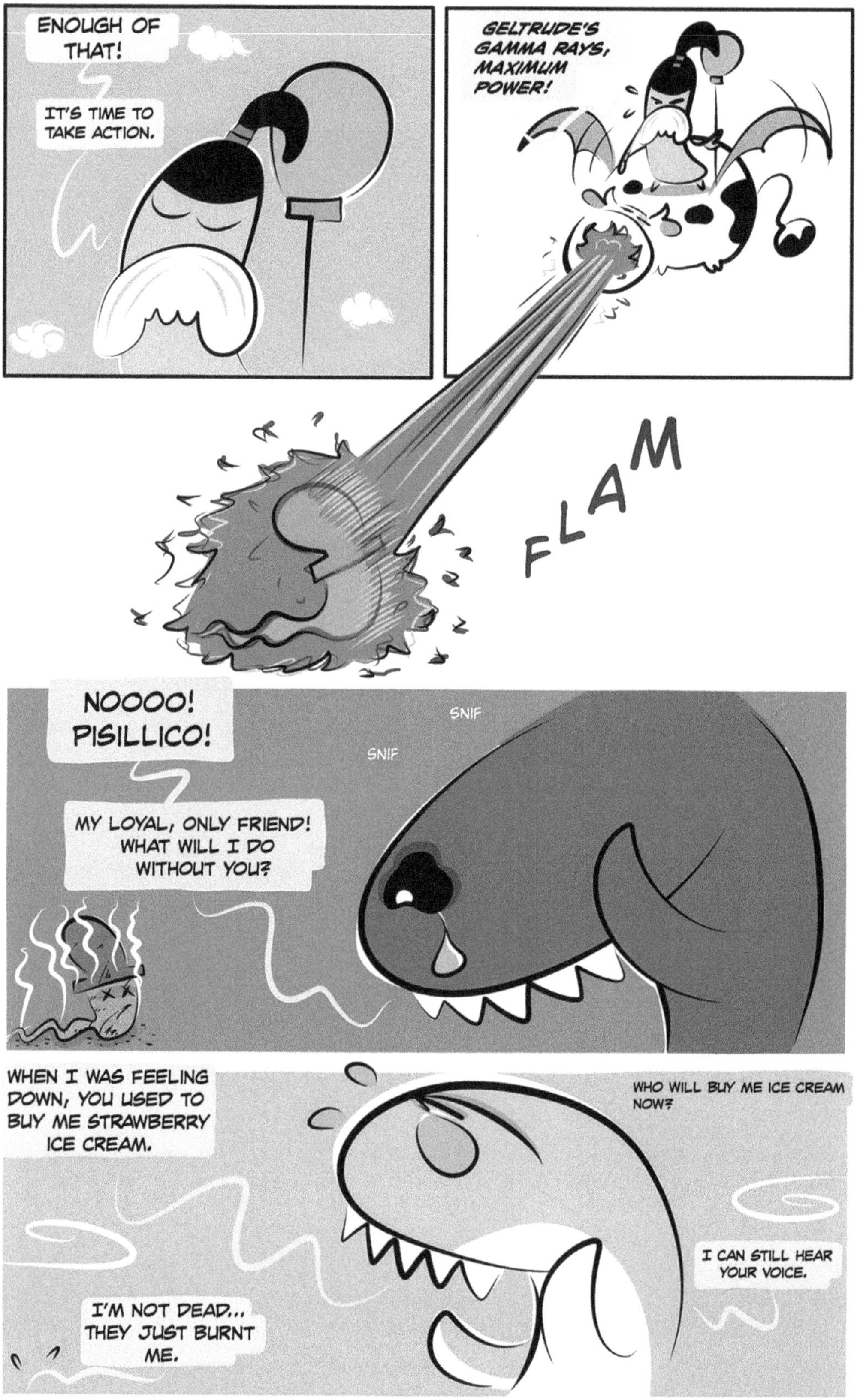
ENOUGH OF THAT!
IT'S TIME TO TAKE ACTION.
GELTRUDE'S GAMMA RAYS, MAXIMUM POWER!
FLAM
NOOOO! PISILLICO!
SNIF
SNIF
MY LOYAL, ONLY FRIEND! WHAT WILL I DO WITHOUT YOU?
WHEN I WAS FEELING DOWN, YOU USED TO BUY ME STRAWBERRY ICE CREAM.
WHO WILL BUY ME ICE CREAM NOW?
I CAN STILL HEAR YOUR VOICE.
I'M NOT DEAD... THEY JUST BURNT ME.

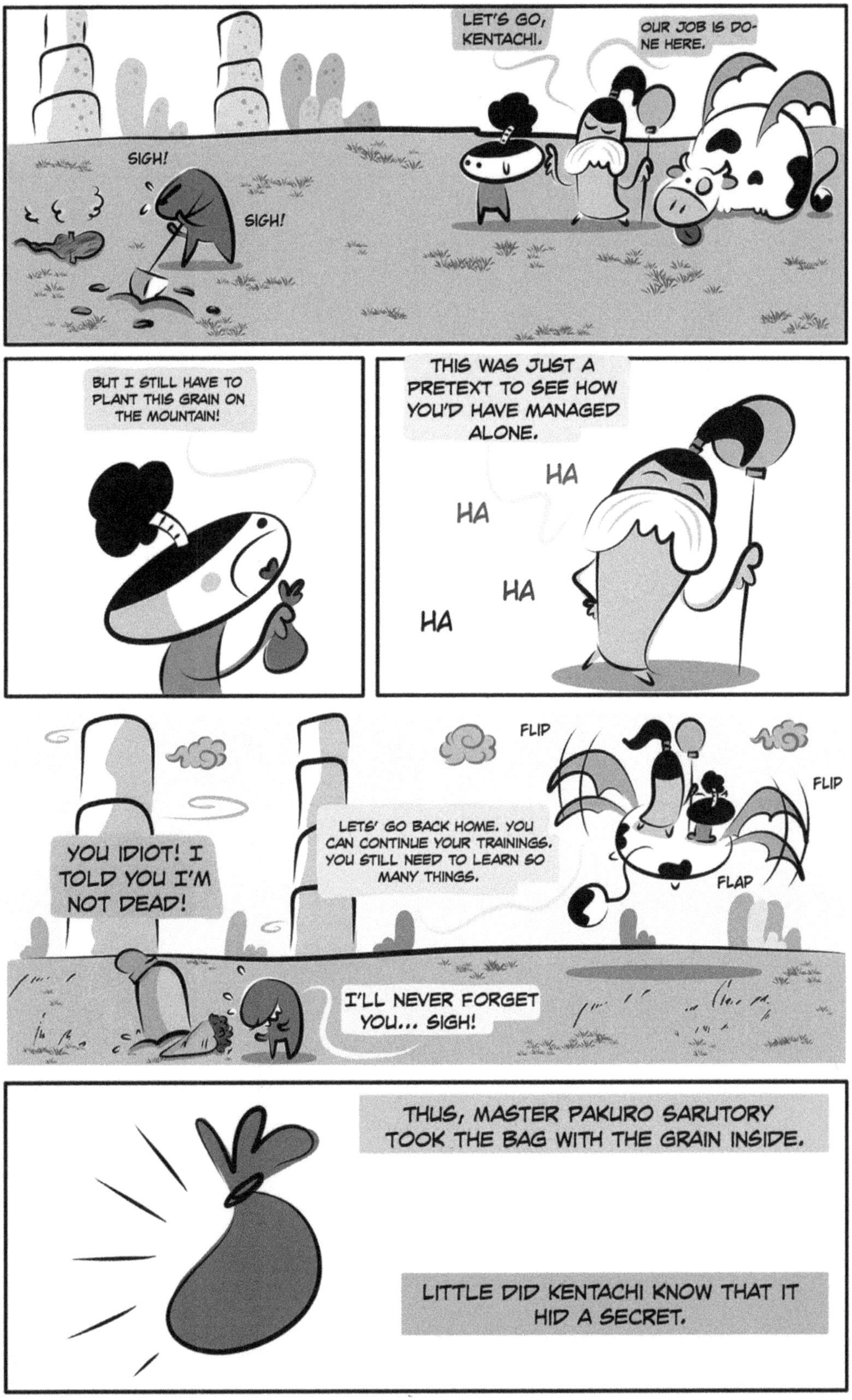
LET'S GO, KENTACHI.
OUR JOB IS DONE HERE.
SIGH!
SIGH!
BUT I STILL HAVE TO PLANT THIS GRAIN ON THE MOUNTAIN!
THIS WAS JUST A PRETEXT TO SEE HOW YOU'D HAVE MANAGED ALONE.
HA
HA
HA
HA
YOU IDIOT! I TOLD YOU I'M NOT DEAD!
LETS' GO BACK HOME. YOU CAN CONTINUE YOUR TRAININGS. YOU STILL NEED TO LEARN SO MANY THINGS.
FLIP
FLIP
FLAP
I'LL NEVER FORGET YOU... SIGH!
THUS, MASTER PAKURO SARUTORY TOOK THE BAG WITH THE GRAIN INSIDE.
LITTLE DID KENTACHI KNOW THAT IT HID A SECRET.

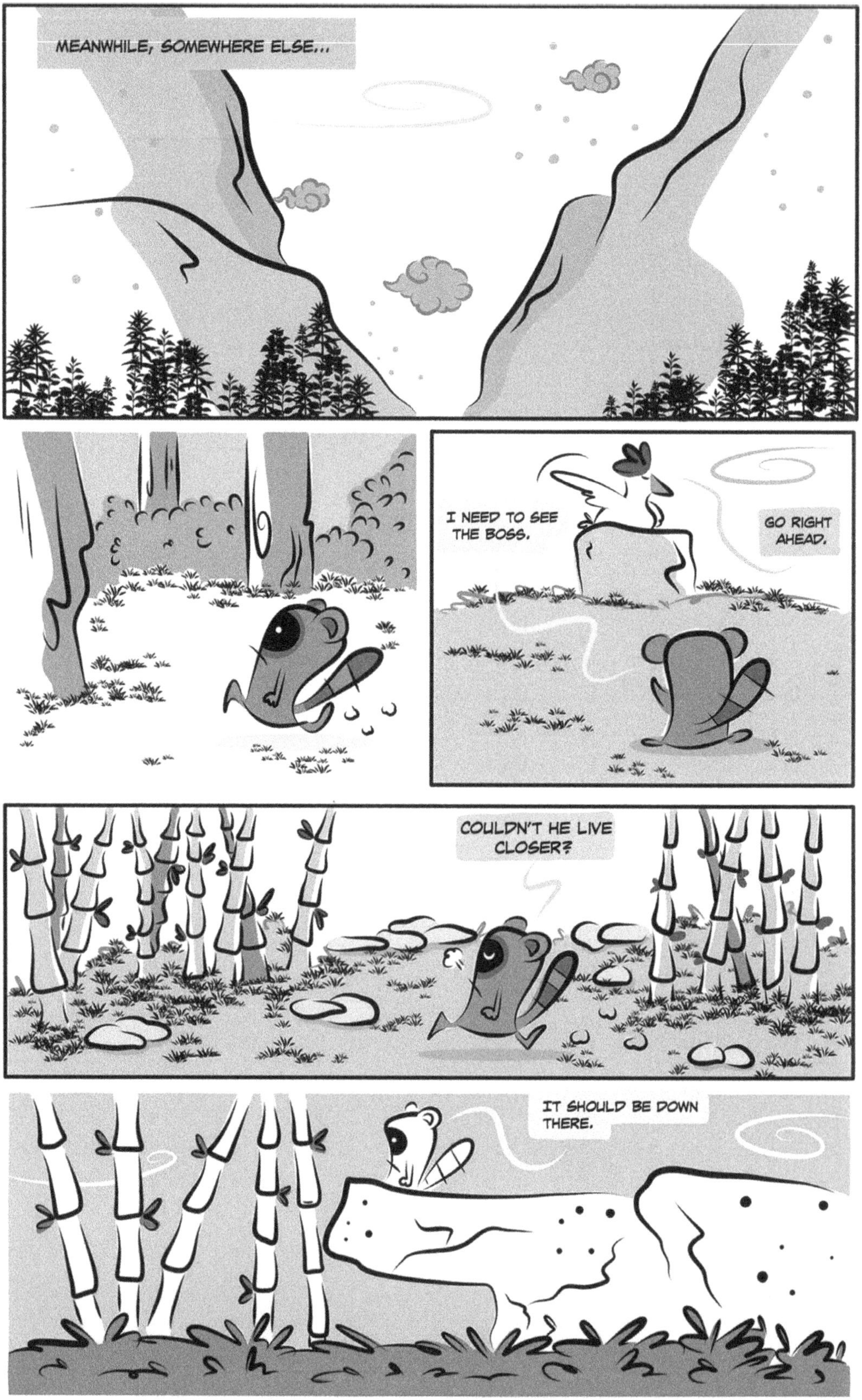
MEANWHILE, SOMEWHERE ELSE...
I NEED TO SEE THE BOSS.
GO RIGHT AHEAD.
COULDN'T HE LIVE CLOSER?
IT SHOULD BE DOWN THERE.

BOSS! BOSS!

I BRING SOME VERY BAD NEWS. MANY OF OUR MEN FAILED OUR MISSION!

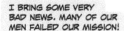

INTERESTING!

FURTHERMORE, I SAW THAT MASTER PAKURO SARUTORY HAS A NEW PUPIL.

BUT I ONLY CARE ABOUT MASTER PAKURO SARUTORY.

LUCKILY ENOUGH, I SUMMONED MEAN LIZARDOLIX OF THE LIZARDAO FAMILY,

ALSO KNOWN AS HUNGRY COBRAS OF THE EAST.

THEY'RE REAL PROS. THEY'VE ALREADY ELIMINATED THREE CLANS, NOT TO MENTION THAT THEY EAT THEIR ENEMIES, AND...

EHI? WHERE DID YOU GO?

AAAHHH!

SLURP

SLURP

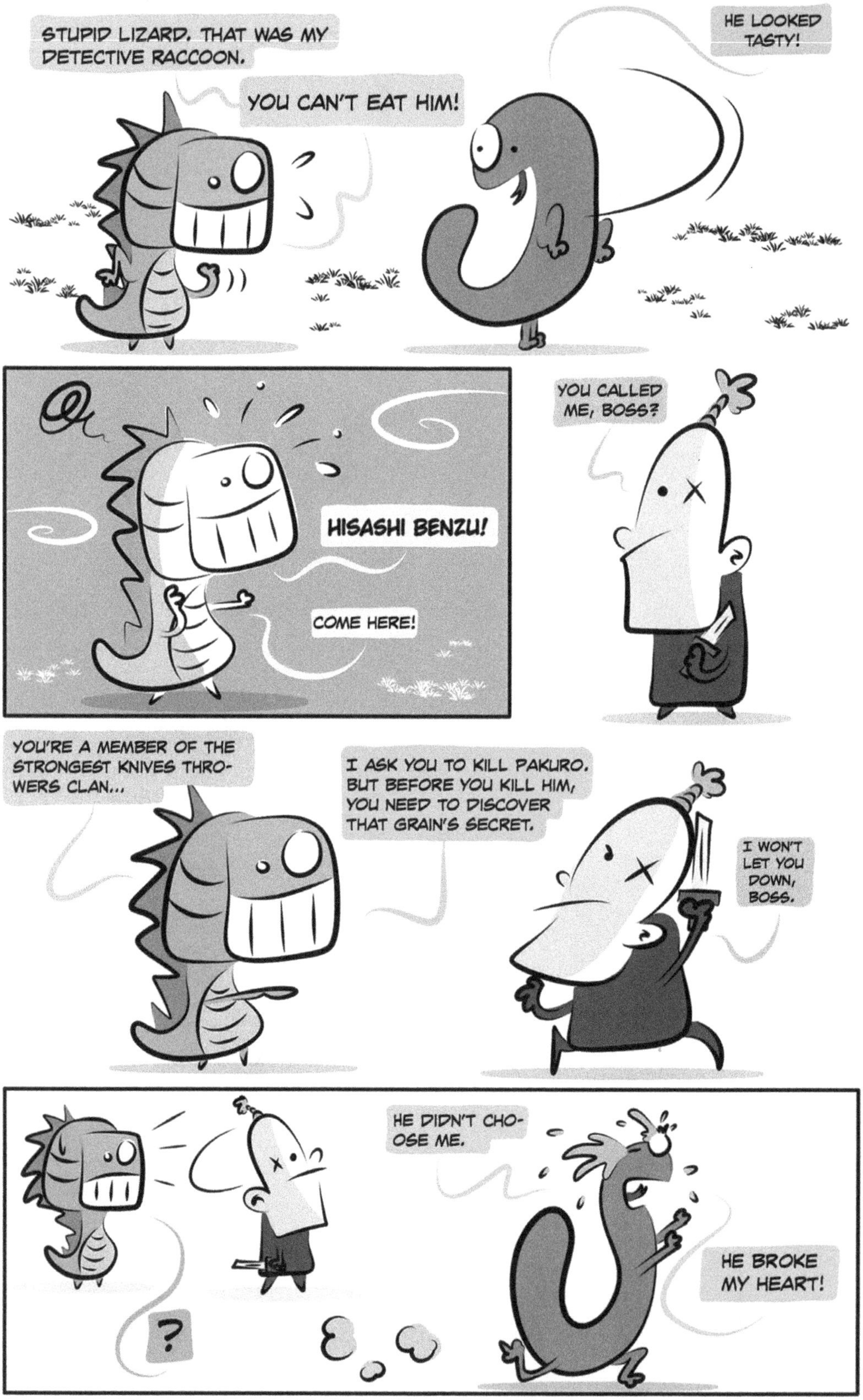
STUPID LIZARD. THAT WAS MY DETECTIVE RACCOON.
YOU CAN'T EAT HIM!
HE LOOKED TASTY!
HISASHI BENZU!
COME HERE!
YOU CALLED ME, BOSS?
YOU'RE A MEMBER OF THE STRONGEST KNIVES THRO-WERS CLAN...
I ASK YOU TO KILL PAKURO. BUT BEFORE YOU KILL HIM, YOU NEED TO DISCOVER THAT GRAIN'S SECRET.
I WON'T LET YOU DOWN, BOSS.
?
HE DIDN'T CHO-OSE ME.
HE BROKE MY HEART!

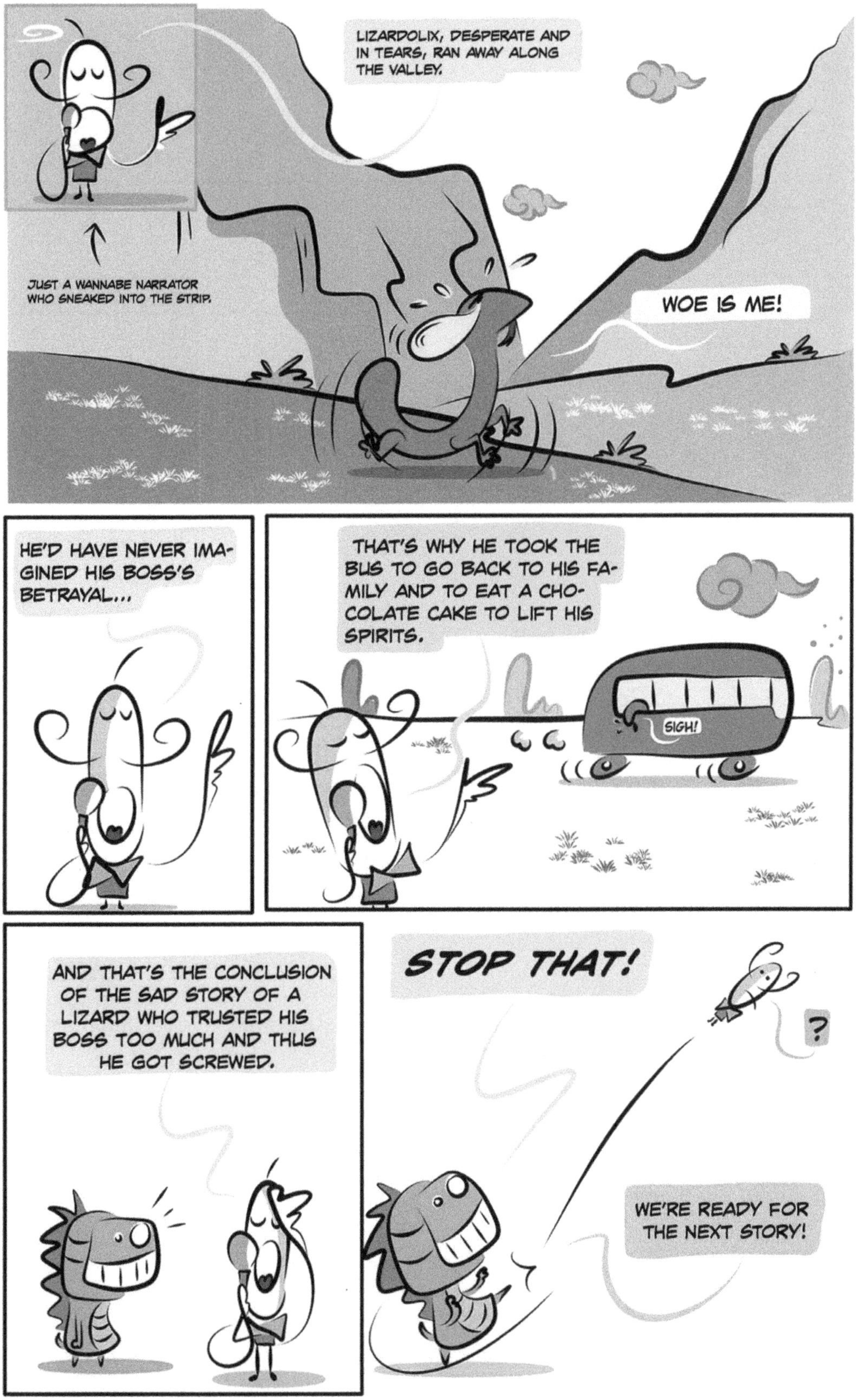
LIZARDOLIX, DESPERATE AND IN TEARS, RAN AWAY ALONG THE VALLEY.
JUST A WANNABE NARRATOR WHO SNEAKED INTO THE STRIP.
WOE IS ME!
HE'D HAVE NEVER IMAGINED HIS BOSS'S BETRAYAL...
THAT'S WHY HE TOOK THE BUS TO GO BACK TO HIS FAMILY AND TO EAT A CHOCOLATE CAKE TO LIFT HIS SPIRITS.
SIGH!
AND THAT'S THE CONCLUSION OF THE SAD STORY OF A LIZARD WHO TRUSTED HIS BOSS TOO MUCH AND THUS HE GOT SCREWED.
STOP THAT!
?
WE'RE READY FOR THE NEXT STORY!

HISASHI
BENZU

LOOK, MASTER! A SWEET CHICK!

KENTACHI, BE CAREFUL!

BOOM

THANK GOD IT DIDN'T HURT YOU! THAT WAS A CHICK BOMB AND I ALSO KNOW...

THAT WAS A CLOSE CALL!

...WHO USES THIS JUTSU!

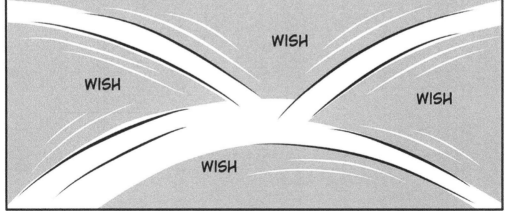

WISH

WISH

WISH

WISH

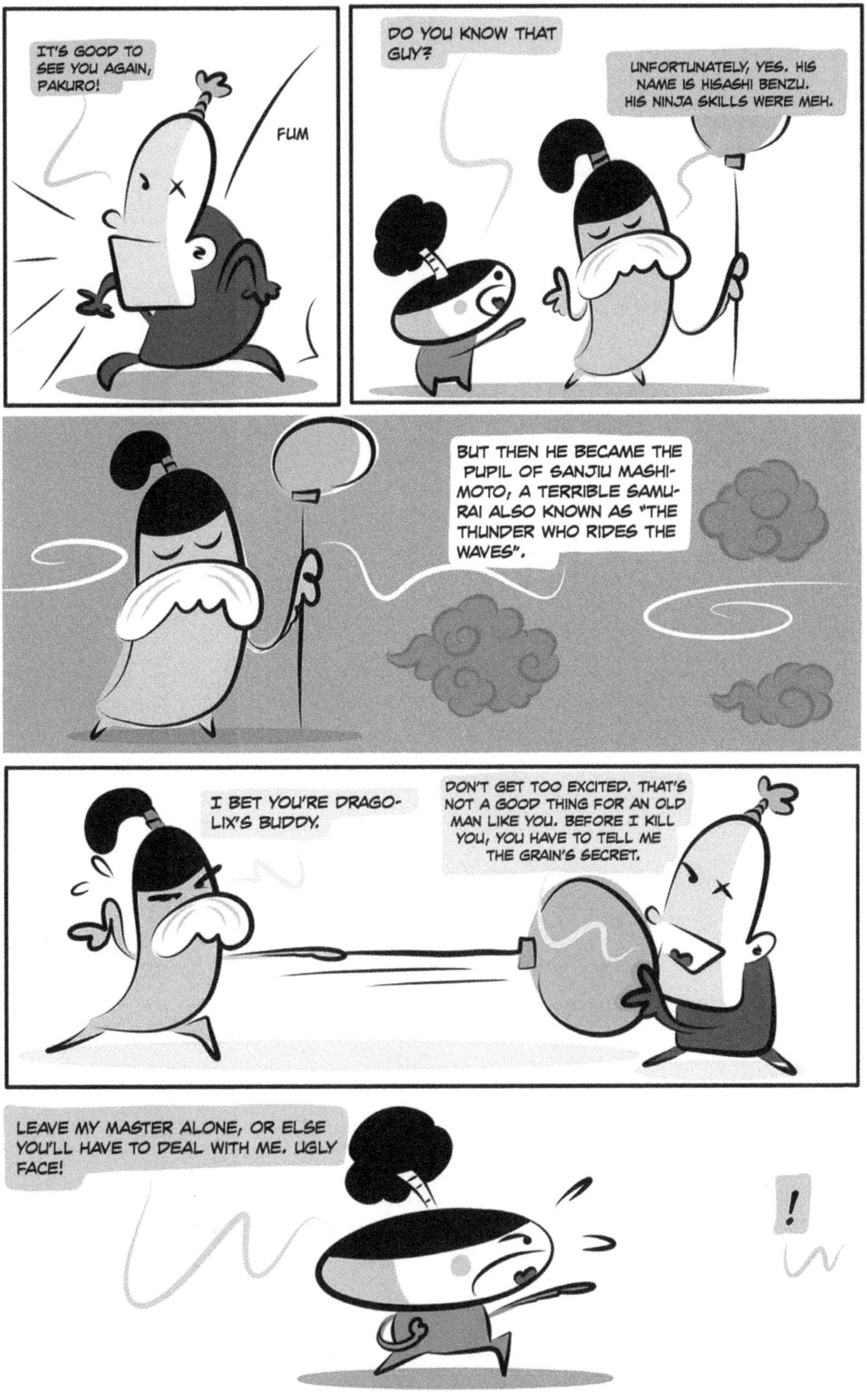
IT'S GOOD TO SEE YOU AGAIN, PAKURO!
FUM
DO YOU KNOW THAT GUY?
UNFORTUNATELY, YES. HIS NAME IS HISASHI BENZU. HIS NINJA SKILLS WERE MEH.
BUT THEN HE BECAME THE PUPIL OF SANJIU MASHI-MOTO, A TERRIBLE SAMU-RAI ALSO KNOWN AS "THE THUNDER WHO RIDES THE WAVES".
I BET YOU'RE DRAGO-LIX'S BUDDY.
DON'T GET TOO EXCITED. THAT'S NOT A GOOD THING FOR AN OLD MAN LIKE YOU. BEFORE I KILL YOU, YOU HAVE TO TELL ME THE GRAIN'S SECRET.
LEAVE MY MASTER ALONE, OR ELSE YOU'LL HAVE TO DEAL WITH ME. UGLY FACE!
!

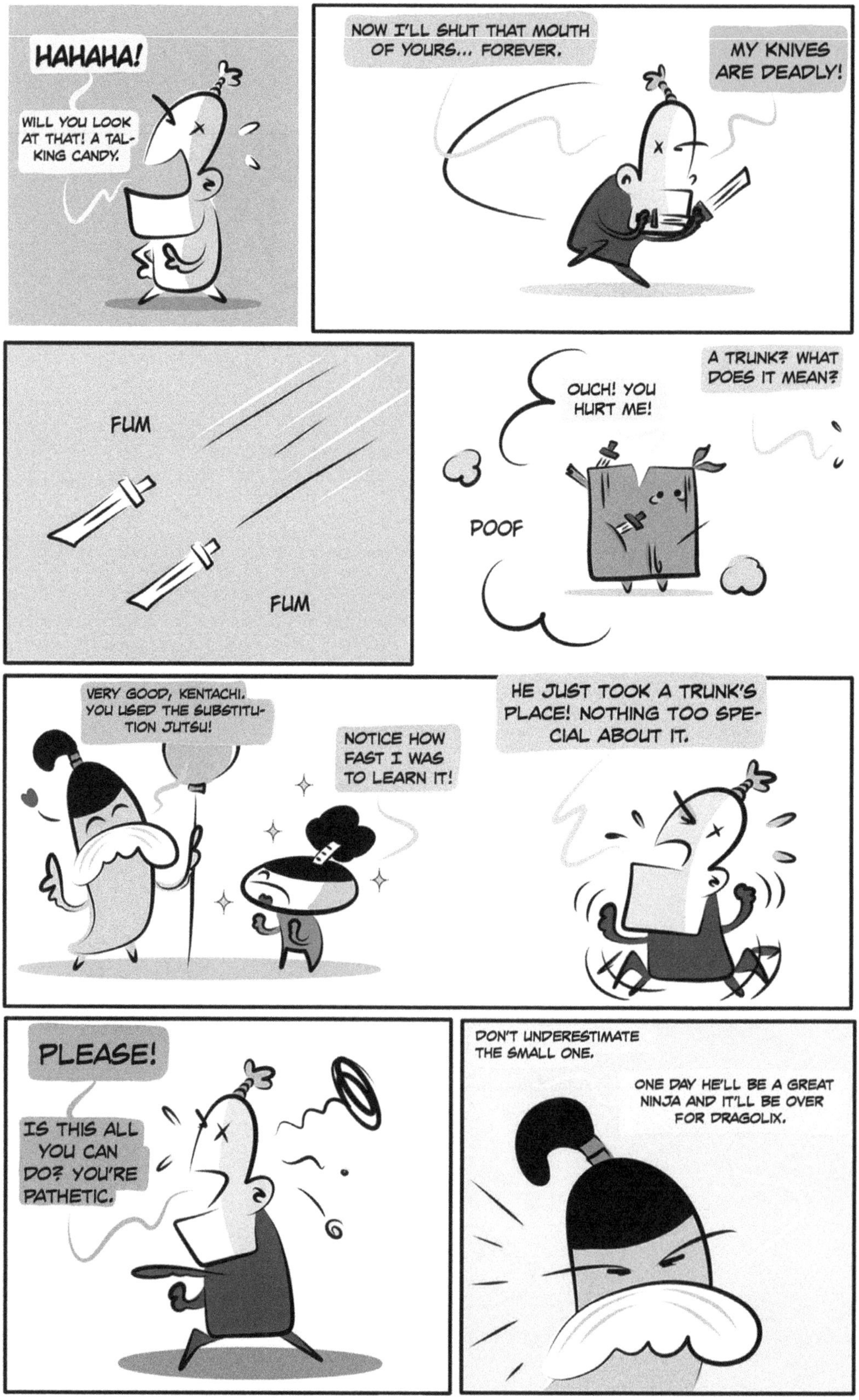
HAHAHA!
WILL YOU LOOK AT THAT! A TAL-KING CANDY.
NOW I'LL SHUT THAT MOUTH OF YOURS... FOREVER.
MY KNIVES ARE DEADLY!
FUM
FUM
A TRUNK? WHAT DOES IT MEAN?
OUCH! YOU HURT ME!
POOF
VERY GOOD, KENTACHI. YOU USED THE SUBSTITU-TION JUTSU!
NOTICE HOW FAST I WAS TO LEARN IT!
HE JUST TOOK A TRUNK'S PLACE! NOTHING TOO SPE-CIAL ABOUT IT.
PLEASE!
IS THIS ALL YOU CAN DO? YOU'RE PATHETIC.
DON'T UNDERESTIMATE THE SMALL ONE.
ONE DAY HE'LL BE A GREAT NINJA AND IT'LL BE OVER FOR DRAGOLIX.

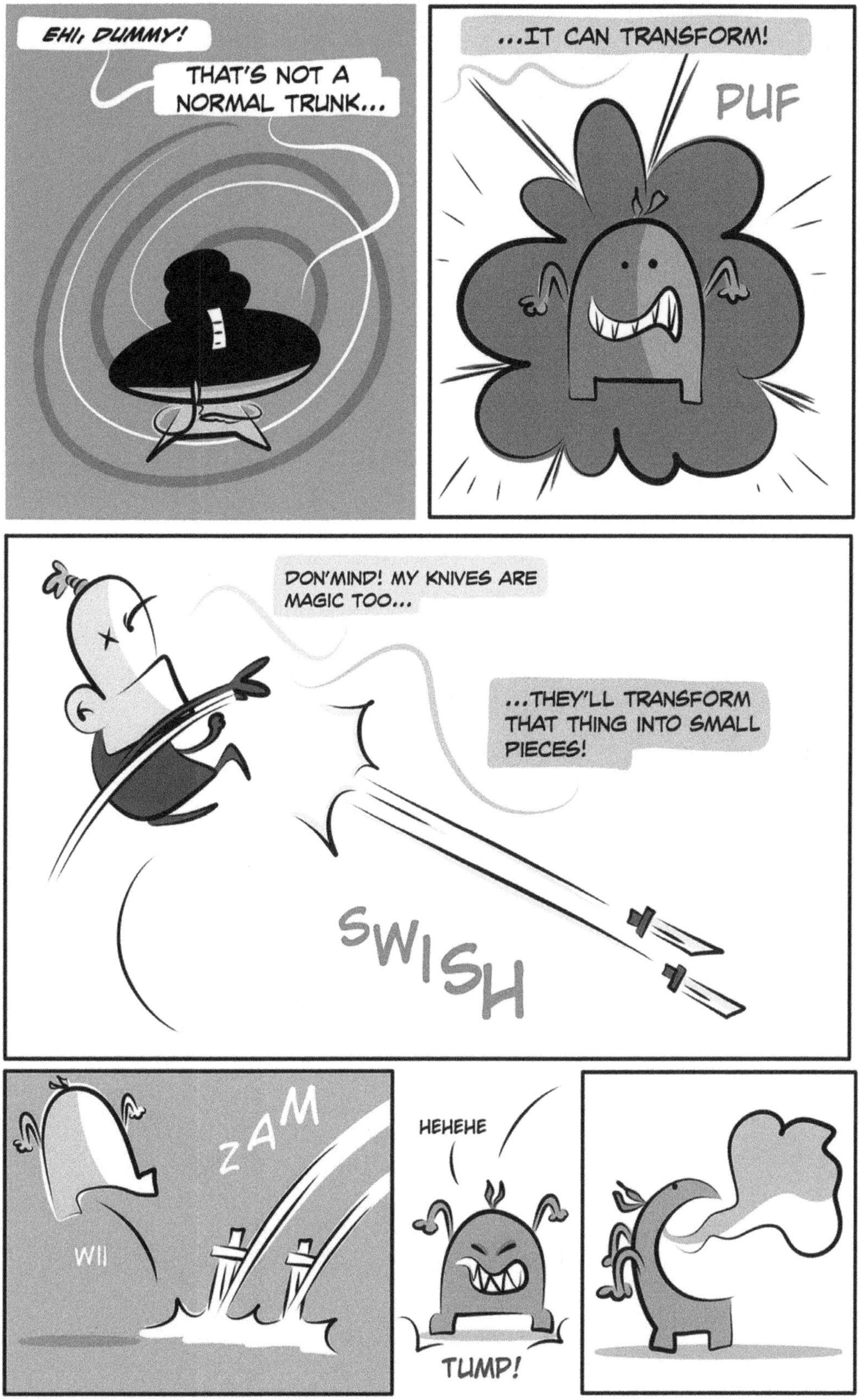
EHI, DUMMY!
THAT'S NOT A NORMAL TRUNK...
...IT CAN TRANSFORM!
PUF
DON'MIND! MY KNIVES ARE MAGIC TOO...
...THEY'LL TRANSFORM THAT THING INTO SMALL PIECES!
SWISH
ZAM
WII
HEHEHE
TUMP!

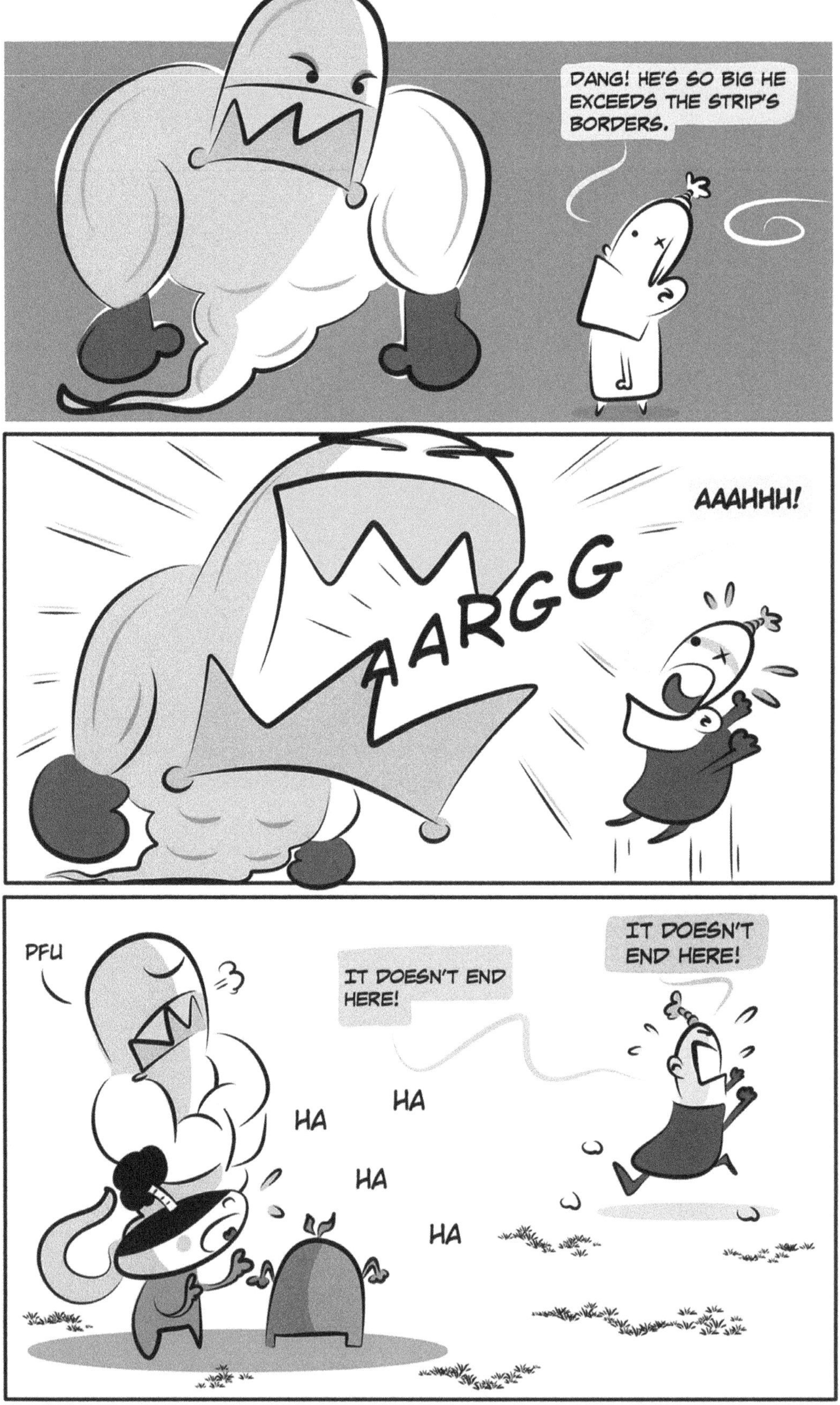
DANG! HE'S SO BIG HE EXCEEDS THE STRIP'S BORDERS.
AAAHHH!
AARGG
PFU
IT DOESN'T END HERE!
IT DOESN'T END HERE!
HA
HA
HA
HA

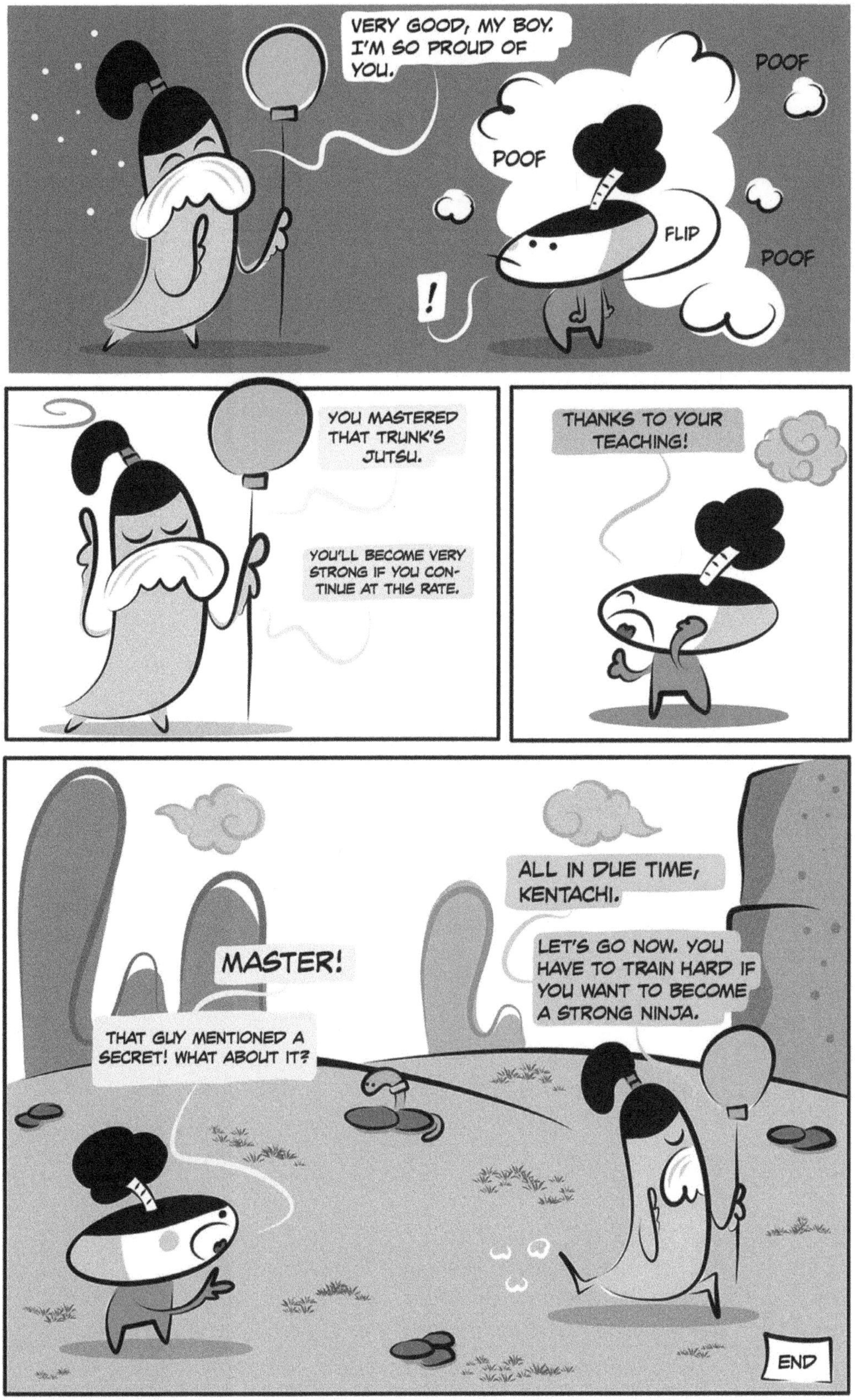
VERY GOOD, MY BOY. I'M SO PROUD OF YOU.
POOF
POOF
FLIP
POOF
!
YOU MASTERED THAT TRUNK'S JUTSU.
YOU'LL BECOME VERY STRONG IF YOU CON-TINUE AT THIS RATE.
THANKS TO YOUR TEACHING!
MASTER!
THAT GUY MENTIONED A SECRET! WHAT ABOUT IT?
ALL IN DUE TIME, KENTACHI.
LET'S GO NOW. YOU HAVE TO TRAIN HARD IF YOU WANT TO BECOME A STRONG NINJA.
END

NAP JUTSU!

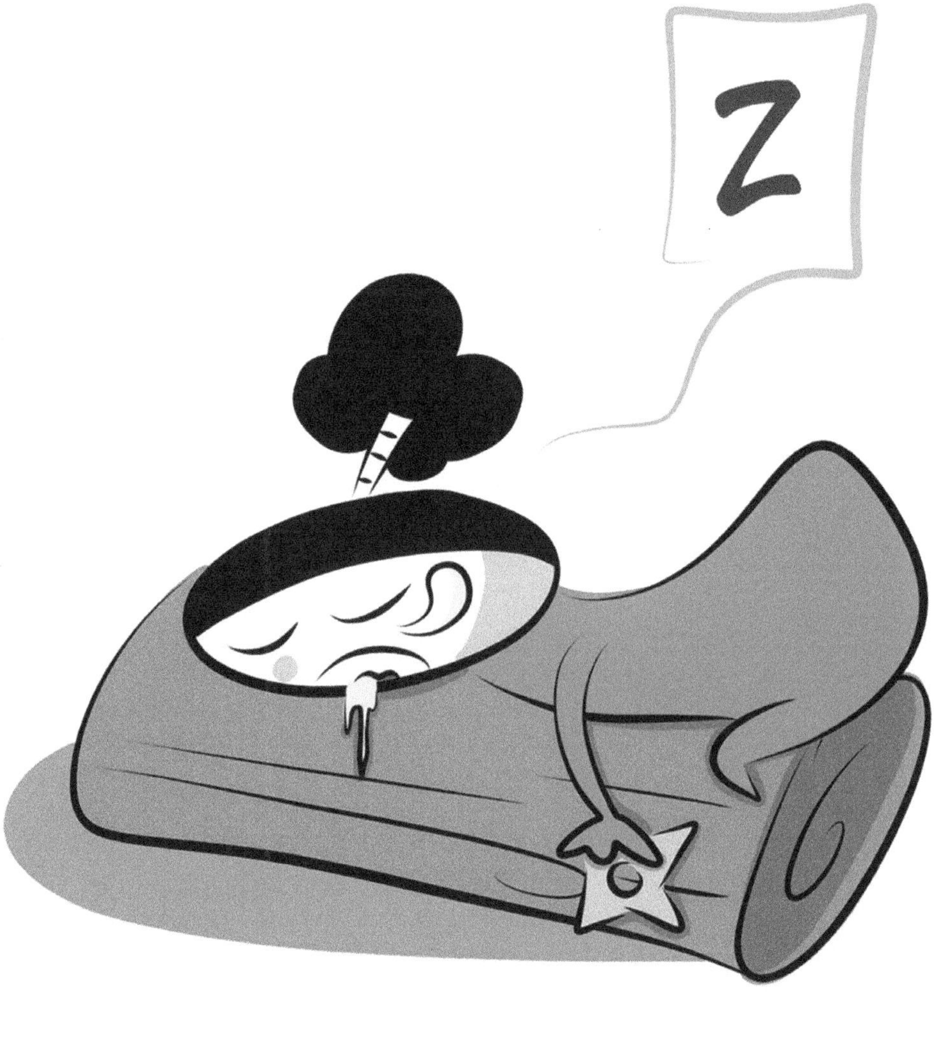
Z

MAKING OF KENTACHI

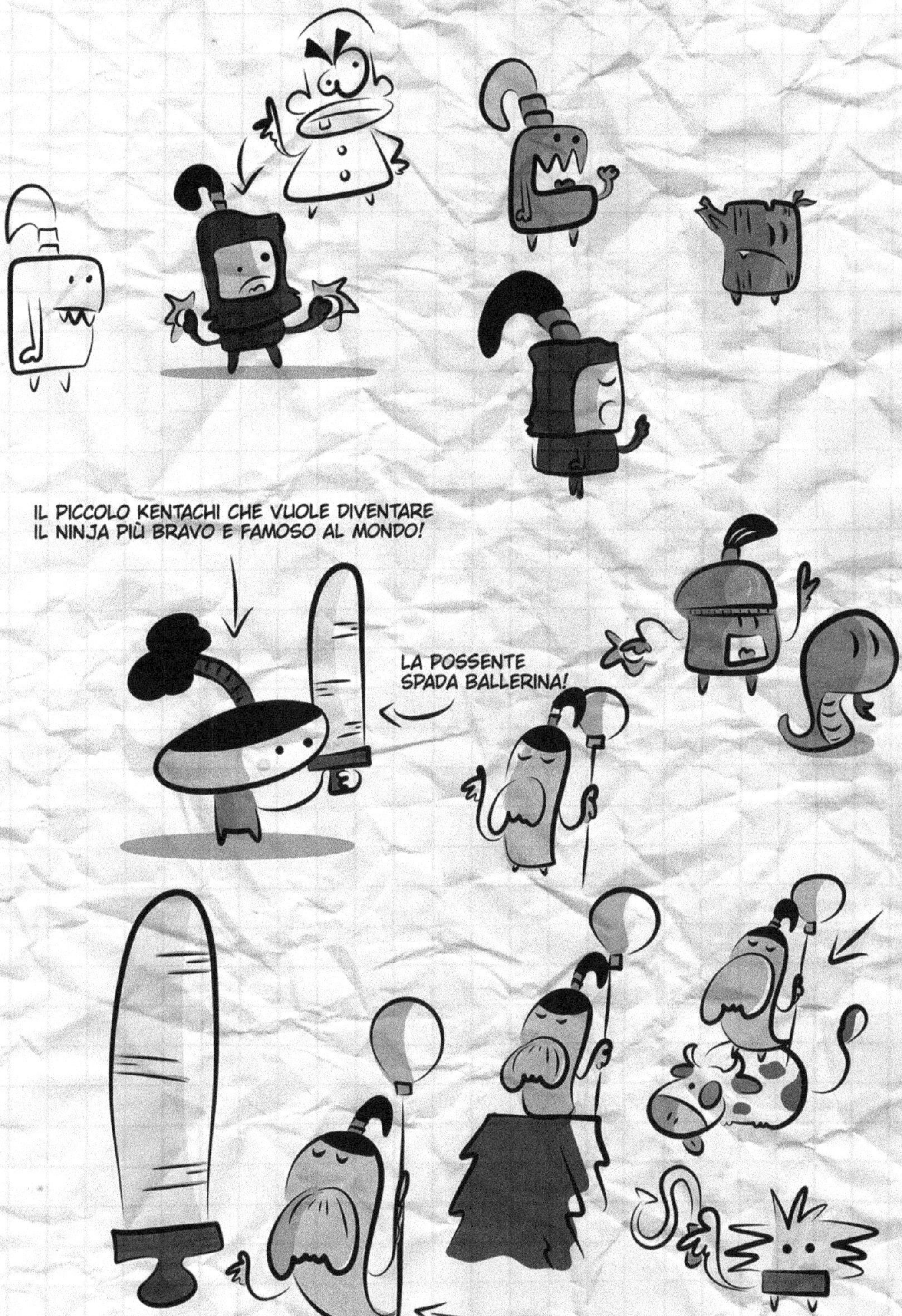

IL PICCOLO KENTACHI CHE VUOLE DIVENTARE
IL NINJA PIÙ BRAVO E FAMOSO AL MONDO!
LA POSSENTE
SPADA BALLERINA!
MAESTRO PAKURO

CHARACTER DESIGN

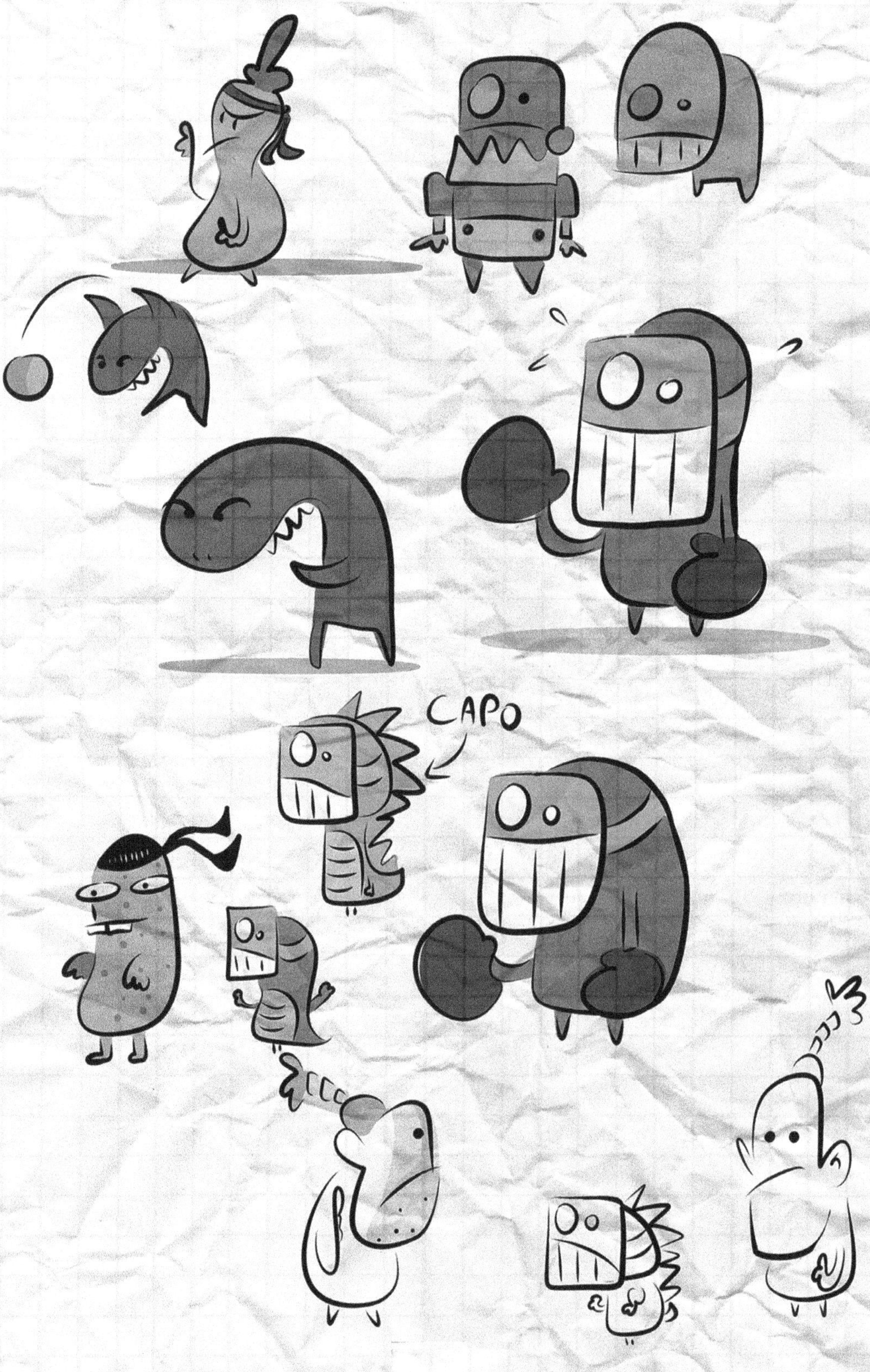
CAPO